W9-BZA-282

"Our country has been at war for all but a few weeks of your high school career. Even before our country was actually in the war, West Technical High School had begun to modify its courses better to meet the war need."

– Principal C.C. Tuck in the
June, 1944 West Tech Yearbook

West Technical High School
Cleveland, Ohio
Circa 1940

ALSO BY PETER JEDICK

League Park

CLEVELAND: Where the East Coast Meets the Midwest

HIPPIES

THE WEST TECH TERRORIST

Peter Jedick

Peter Jedick Enterprises

Rocky River, Ohio

Copyright © 2007 by Peter Jedick

No part of this book may be reproduced in any manner without the written permission of the author, except in brief quotations used in articles and reviews.

This is a work of fiction. Names, characters, places and incidents either are the product of the author's imagination or are used fictitiously, and any resemblance to actual persons, living or dead, business establishments, events, or locales is entirely coincidental. Principal C.C. Tuck and Safety Director Eliot Ness are fictional portrayals of historic personalities.

The West Tech Terrorist is published by:

Peter Jedick Enterprises
22470 Blossom Drive
Rocky River, Ohio 44116

First edition, July, 2007

For information contact www.westtechterrorist.com

Cover design by Denise Ziganti of Design Direction
(www.designdirection.biz)

Cover illustration by Louis Grasso

Interior design by Ben Small of Grafik Dezine

Alma Mater song photo by Tim Ryan

Other photos courtesy of
The West Tech Alumni Association
P.O. Box 110231
Cleveland, Ohio 44111-0231
www.westtech.org

ISBN: 978-0-9605508-4-5
Library of Congress Control Number: 2007904416

Printed by Fine Line Litho, Cleveland, Ohio, USA

This book is dedicated to my father, Peter Jedick, West Tech class of January, 1942. He parachuted into France on D-Day during World War II with the 101st Airborne Division.

It is also dedicated to Charles Dietrich, my journalism teacher and *West Tech Tatler* advisor.

TABLE OF CONTENTS

THE WEST TECH TERRORIST

DEAR OLD WEST TECH
(Alma Mater Song)

Dear old West Tech, we'll always love you,

Sure as the stars do shine above you.

Always loyal and always true,

We love you more every day.

Down through the years we'll all be yearning

To these dear old halls to be returning.

Dear old, WEST TECH, we're all for you,

For the crimson and gray!

The Prologue

It was a hot, humid August night in Cleveland, Ohio. The year was 1941. Three friends from West Tech High school had decided to take a night swim in Lake Erie at Edgewater Beach, just west of downtown. Officially the beach closed at 9 p.m. and thousands of swimmers were headed back to the sweltering city streets.

It was only a few days before Labor Day weekend and school would start again the Tuesday after the holiday. The boys thought they would have one last summer fling before they started their senior year.

Sneaking into the park after hours was not hard. There were still many swimmers and picnickers strolling around the park, enjoying the cool Lake Erie breezes. A few night fishermen dotted the rocky piers jutting out into the waves.

Swimming in the water was a different story. The lifeguards who patrolled the lakefront frowned on swimming after sunset, it made their job almost impossible. But the boys had an in, one of their friends from West Tech was working that day, and he looked the other way as they slipped into the water unobserved.

Quietly they stroked out to the deep water, beyond the noise on the shore. The water was cool and peaceful and the boys forgot the many worries of the day. Despite their young years their generation was shouldering a large load of responsibilities.

The United States was just beginning to recover from the misery of the Great Depression. Jobs would be scarce when they graduated from high school. Their families were struggling to put food on their tables. And war clouds were gathering in Europe that might change everything. So they floated on their backs, looked up at the stars and said little, not wanting to be noticed.

Suddenly, they heard a noise in the darkness, like a school of fish thrashing about. But as they listened the sound grew louder and they could hear voices above the din speaking in a foreign language.

It was a boat moving swiftly toward them. They had to duck under the waves to avoid being hit with the props from the outboard motor. It happened so quickly the boys did not know what to make of the ruckus. The boat should have had a light on its bow but it did not. Then it stopped moving for a few moments and two bodies jumped in the water and began swimming to shore. The two strangers still remaining in the boat, turned it around and headed back toward the deep water. In a flash the vessel was gone, as quickly as it appeared.

The three West Tech students did not know what to make of the incident. They could not recognize the foreign dialect or make out any of the words above the noise of the motor. That was not unusual since Cleveland in the 1940s was a melting pot and many citizens were European immigrants, like their parents, who did not speak English.

But the stealth of the operation did make them curious. There were no lights on the boat and no sign of a bigger boat that might have deposited it in the water. It was a dangerous operation considering the amount of boat traffic on Lake Erie.

However, they were high school kids and easily distracted. The boys soon went back to floating on their backs. They discussed the strange sight for a few minutes then their conversation moved on to other subjects like girls and sports. By the time they snuck out of the water and walked back home they began to forget that the incident ever occurred.

CHAPTER ONE:
The National Air Races

Labor Day weekend in Cleveland, Ohio, always meant one thing. The National Air Races. And in 1941, with the country on the brink of war, there was greater interest than usual.

The National Air Races were held at Cleveland Municipal Airport, on the southwest outskirts of the city. There were two types of races, one a long distance race that originated on the west coast and local races that started and ended at the airport.

In the local races the planes would fly in a long course around the airport, marked by pylons that jutted up into the sky. The planes would screech and howl as they cut around the pylons much like the horses in the Kentucky Derby or the cars in the Indianapolis 500.

And the long distance races were just as popular an event. It was even broadcast live across the country through the magic of radio.

For one glorious weekend Cleveland was the toast of the nation. It was such a big affair that it attracted thousands of spectators, many from other states. Hollywood movie stars and captains of industry converged on the city to watch the drama and witness the latest advances in aviation technology.

The Air Races also served a practical purpose. Many of the pilots built their own planes and used old-fashioned American ingenuity to develop new innovations. Their ideas often resulted in changes to both commercial and military airplanes.

So it was not unusual to find three students from Cleveland's West Tech High School sitting on a hill near the airport runways. They were enjoying the warm fresh air while watching the planes take off and land. Ed Gorski, Frank Roulette, and my self, Victor Blazek, biked all the way from the near west side of Cleveland to join in the festivities. It was a good ten-mile trek but well worth the effort.

The reason we were sitting on a hill is that we could not afford to buy tickets to sit in the grandstands. It was the same reason we did not take Frank's 1936 Dodge coupe. Even if we could scrape together enough cash to pay for the gasoline, we did not have the gas coupons needed to purchase it. Gasoline was already being rationed in preparation for the United States entering the war in Europe.

However, there was an upside to using our bicycles. While we were not as close as the paying customers sitting in the grandstands, we had a much better view than the many Cleveland citizens who parked their cars around the perimeter of the airport.

Our hilltop view was phenomenal for the price, free. Small fighter planes like the new Curtiss P-40 roared right over our heads. Large passenger planes taxied on the runways below us. We could even watch the huge B-17 bombers take off. They were built right next to the airport at Cleveland's bomber plant.

The U.S. Army Air Force was building them to send to Great Britain where the English were trying to defend their homeland from the advances of Adolf Hitler's Nazi Germany. But we were not naïve. We knew England and France were hoping to bring the United States into the war on their side and when it happened we would soon be fighting the Germans.

"I'd love to get my hands on one of those P-40 engines," Frank said, stretching his long legs out in front of him. Frank majored in aircraft engine repair at Tech and loved rubbing his greasy hands on anyone who came near him. At six foot three inches tall he stood head and shoulders above the rest of us, the general population being much shorter back then. He was also the starting forward on the Carpenter's basketball team. We called him "Fly-boy" or "Ace" because of his desire to become a fighter pilot.

"Why, so you could wreck it?" Ed looked over at him, sitting on his crossed legs. Gorski was almost as wide as Roulette was tall. He was a drafting major and star halfback on the football team. As close friends we called him "Stash" because of his Polish background. But most of the students at Tech knew him as "T-square," which was a drafting instrument used in mechanical drawing. The class was a basic requirement for all the male students at Tech.

"Nah," I said. "He'd probably soup it up like his old jalopy, add a hundred miles an hour to its speed. " I liked to defend Frank from Ed's constant jabs although I did enjoy the banter. Chemistry was my major at Tech and I was on the wrestling team, although without much success.

They called me "Slats" after the skinny pieces of wood we used in our carpentry classes. For the life of me, no matter how much I ate, I could not add a few pounds to my skinny frame. My wrestling teammates spent hours in tents made by throwing blankets over the hot water pipes in Tech's basement attempting to lose weight for their matches. They hated my overactive metabolism.

"No, I'd just like to tear it apart, see how it ticks," Frank explained. "Those babies are way ahead of the ancient Pratt-Whitney's we get to play with at Tech."

"You should have majored in auto shop. They don't have carburetors on bomber engines. Hey, here comes a racer." Ed jumped to his feet and pointed his finger up to the sky. A gold, single motor aircraft was coming straight for us, only a few hundred feet over our heads.

We jumped up with him. "That's Roscoe Turner," Frank said. As the plane approached we could see the world famous aviator sitting in the open cockpit, his white scarf blowing in the wind just like in a photo from World War I.

We waved at him and he looked down at us, giving us a salute from the top of his leather cap. Then he tipped his wing at the crowd and did a loop-de-loop right above it. The fans in the grandstands cheered wildly.

"I want to do that someday," Frank said.

"Fly Turner's airplane? I don't think he'll let you in the pilot's seat," Ed said.

"I don't think you'd fit. Your legs are too long," I added.

"I don't care whose plane it is, I just want to fly." Frank spread out his long arms like a condor and made engine sounds with his mouth.

"Then you better join the Air Corps before the Infantry grabs you," I laughed. The United States had just started the first peacetime draft in the nation's history, anticipating entering the war in Europe.

"Yeah, the Air Force will give you free lessons," Ed added. "If you don't mind being shot down by a German Messerschmitt."

"What do you know, you pencil pusher," Frank shot back.

"If I were you I'd stick to fixing them," I said. "A lot safer, buddy."

"No, once they see how he fixes them, they'll put him in the cockpit right away," Ed continued his verbal attack.

"Someday I'll be riding the winds while you guys are marching in the mud, looking up at me," Frank continued. "Eat your hearts out."

"The Air Show's winding down. I think we should be heading home," I said, hoping to break up the shots before they became personal.

"Yeah, it's getting dark." Ed started walking down the hill and we followed him.

Our hill was situated between the airport and the bomber plant so as we descended Frank came up with an idea.

"How about if we swing by the bomber plant and try to catch a glimpse of a B-17?"

"Just for a second. It'll be dark soon and I hate biking in the dark," Ed said.

"Why, you chicken?" Frank asked.

"No, I just hate those drivers who don't give you a break. They act like they own the road."

We jumped on our bikes and raced down the bumpy hill. A few hundred feet from the bottom was a cyclone fence with a barbed wire top that circled around the grounds of the bomber plant. There was a path that paralleled the fence, probably left there by security vehicles that patrolled the perimeter. We followed it along the back of the huge concrete structure.

You cannot imagine the immensity of the bomber plant unless you walk inside it when it is empty. It takes your breath away, almost like seeing the Grand Canyon for the first time. Consider how much room it takes to house an Air Force bomber and then multiply it by ten.

We decided to bike over to the side of the plant where the doors were located. It is where the planes were taken out for fine tuning before they taxied on the runway. If we were lucky we might spot one sitting on the concrete platform. It would make Frank's day.

We biked through a wooded area and were just about to come to another opening when we saw a couple of men standing by the fence. One of them had a black box hanging around his neck. It looked like a camera and it was pointed at the bomber plant.

When they heard us coming one of them started to move away very quickly. But the one with the camera grabbed him by the arm and made him stay.

We hit the brakes and pulled up beside them. As we did, our eyes followed the direction of their camera. A big B-17 Flying Fortress bomber was parked a hundred yards away from us.

"How you boys doing?" the cameraman asked in a thick accent. It was definitely Eastern European and if I had to guess based on my limited knowledge of Cleveland's many dialects I would have said Austrian. "That's a fine piece of machinery."

We dismounted our bikes. "No shit," Ed said, expressing our sentiments exactly.

"No sheet?" the Austrian laughed. "What eez that?"

"It means it is a fine piece of machinery," Frank answered.

The huge bomber was glistening in the late summer sunshine. Its shiny silver metal and huge black tires reminded me of a new car sitting in a showroom, not that I'd ever driven one but I did like to look at them.

"Victor Blazek," I held out my hand in the spirit of friendship with an obvious foreigner.

"Blazek, eh? Is that Czech?"

"No Russian. And you are?"

The cameraman looked at his partner before answering. "Austrian," he said.

"I meant your name."

"Oh, Heinrich Henzeldorph."

"Why the camera?" Frank suddenly asked with an air of suspicion that I did not understand.

"Oh, we come to air show to watch airplanes, take pictures for wife. She loves planes, too."

"The Air Show is over that way," Frank pointed north.

"Of course, we take pictures of those planes. We wanted to look at the famous bomber much like yourself." You could tell old Heinrich was forcing the cordial reply. "Time to go, Olaf?" he pointed at his watch

"Yah," Olaf nodded. His silence during the conversation implied that he did not understand English.

"Auf wiedersehen," said the Austrian. The two men waved and trudged back up into the wooded hillside.

Ed and I waved a friendly goodbye but Frank kept a wary eye on them.

"I didn't like the looks of those two," he said.

"Why, what's wrong with them? I asked.

"They look like spies to me," Frank said.

"You've been listening to too many episodes of The Shadow," Ed laughed.

"Then what's with the camera?"

"My brother has a dark room in our basement," I said. "Does that make him a spy?"

"If he's taking pictures of B-17's for who knows what country then I say check him out."

"Do you want to follow them?" I asked.

"No, it's getting too late. But we should report those guys to the FBI."

"You handle it, Ace," Ed said. "I'm getting hungry. Let's head for home."

We all agreed but not before stopping for one last look at that immense weapon of mass destruction, the B-17 bomber.

"Mark my words, I'm going to fly me one of those babies," Frank dreamed out loud as we saddled up for our long ride home.

CHAPTER TWO:
The Tatler

It was ninth period, my last class of the day, and I was hanging around *The Tatler* office. *The Tatler* was the West Tech student newspaper. It came out once a week and the office was located in room 106.

Working on *The Tatler* was one of the few breaks you earned at Dear Old West Tech, a high school famous for its discipline. If you worked on the school paper you could take it as an elective English class. It always met eighth and ninth periods, the last two classes of the school day.

Room 106 was pretty sloppy by West Tech standards. It resembled a big city newspaper office. Some of the desks had typewriters on them. Paper was scattered everywhere. The latest *Tatler* issue was pinned up on a bulletin board along with famous newspaper articles like THE STOCK MARKET CRASH OF 1929. Piles of back issues were stacked on the large windowsill, the windows looking out over the track and football field. That was my domain.

I was the Sports Editor back in September, 1941. That seems so long ago now. We were all hot about taking on the Nazis and making the world safe for democracy, ideals that don't carry much weight nowadays.

Mr. Friedrich was our faculty advisor. He was always trying to assign stories to me that were not sports related. I guess he was trying to broaden my horizons, prepare me for college, but I was not buying into it. Everyone knew it was just a matter of time before the United States was dragged into the war in Europe. I knew I'd be drafted as soon as I graduated if I didn't enlist into one of the armed services. College was light years away, if ever.

So my attitude was *que sera, sera*, whatever will be, will be. Live for today, for tomorrow you may be gone. I liked sports, all of them, but the only one I was any good at was wrestling and who cared about that sport. Lots of pain, no fans, no glory, no cash. So once I discovered that I could write a lick I figured it would keep me in the game so to speak.

But here comes old Mr. Friedrich, walking right up to me with a *Cleveland Press* rolled up in his hand. I knew he was up to something.

"Victor, I have an idea for you," he said in his rough German accent. He always had ideas for me.

"What would that be, sir?" I asked as politely as possible. I closed my English textbook that was wrapped around a Superman comic. Technically we were not allowed to read comics in the classroom. Mr. Friedrich was a bit more liberal than most Tech teachers when it came to my literary tastes but there was no use rubbing it in his face.

"Did you see the story in *The Press* on our own Mr. Fleming?" he asked me. "How come we missed this?"

"Probably because it's only a few paragraphs buried in the back of the paper," I surmised as he opened an old edition of *The Cleveland Press* on my desk.

The small headline read LOCAL TEACHER TAPPED BY WAR DEPARTMENT FOR RESEARCH WORK.

I quickly scanned the story. It seemed that our distinguished chemistry teacher was going to help out the government. The details were sketchy but it had something to do with creating man-made chemicals.

"Not 'why we didn't see it?'" he explained. "Why did we not write this first?"

"Because Mr. Fleming is a modest man?"

"Whatever the reason, we blew it. And since a voracious reader like yourself missed it in *The Press* it is our duty to inform our 4500 students about our esteemed colleague."

"I don't know about voracious." I offered my own small dose of humility.

"You can't fool me, Mr. Blazek, I know you read more than just the sports page and the comics."

"When I have the time."

"Why don't you go visit Mr. Fleming and see if you can

add to this story?" he handed me his copy of *The Press*.

"I don't know, there's the big football game Friday night against Lakewood. That's going to keep me pretty busy. Why don't you give it to Maria? She loves to brown-nose the teachers."

"That's exactly why I'd rather you do it. It'll be a simple story, not much more than a rewrite. You just have to be careful not to plagiarize."

"Plagiarize?"

"You can't take any quotes directly from *The Press* story. You have to rewrite them and add your own angle. Maybe ask him some personal things about teaching at Tech. *The Press* was more interested in his research, especially the potential for weaponry."

"Weaponry?" I missed that angle.

"Caught your attention, Mr. Blazek?"

"Yeah, I guess. Maybe I can find the time." I tried not to appear too excited even though I was. Never volunteer for anything, that was my motto. I was preparing myself for the Army.

"Try to have it to me by Friday, then you can do the football story Monday."

"How many words?"

"Two hundred will be plenty."

"Can I have a hall pass?"

"You are interested."

"I might as well get it over with," I shrugged.

CHAPTER THREE:
Chemistry Class

I took Mr. Friedrich's handwritten hall pass and shoved it deep into my pants pocket. Then I walked out into the quiet hallway. *The Tatler* office was located in the northwest corner of the school. The chemistry classes were on the third floor so I should have just darted up the northwest staircase. But it was hard for me to pass up an opportunity to mess with "Mousey." So I decided to take the scenic route and use the northeast stairway instead. That would take me right past Mousey's domain.

Mousey sat in front of the stairs by the front entrance to the school and the principal's office. She was one of only two security guards in the entire West Tech high school. She was nicknamed Mousey because of the strange hairdo sitting on top of her head.

Mousey was not much of a security guard by today's standards. She was five feet one inches tall and weighed about ninety-eight pounds. She didn't carry a gun or a nightstick or a walkie-talkie. She didn't have to. All she had to do was finger you and look out. The whole weight of the school administration came down on you. I'll tell you about Principal C. C. Tuck later. Let's just say he had ways with the students that the Nazis wished they had invented.

Anyway, I loved rattling Mousey's cage. The hallway was amazingly quiet and empty for ninth period. Did I mention that West Tech was the largest high school in the state of Ohio? That some claimed it was the second largest high school in the country?

The huge four story structure housed over 4500 students. That's why the strong discipline was so important. If that many students ever lost control, look out.

There I was walking down a hallway that was so quiet that I could hear my own footsteps. Army green-colored lockers lined every inch of wall space. The red clay tile floors were shiny. The overhead lights hanging from black metal rods glowed brightly. And there was Mousey giving me the evil eye.

You see, a normal West Tech hall pass was huge. Take the auto shop, for example. It used a hubcap from an old Packard. The wood shop burned its room number into a polished slice of oak. The foundry's was a hunk of iron that weighed a ton. Even the regular classrooms, like English in room 222, were works of art put together by one technical class or another.

That's the way West Tech functioned. It was a little world unto itself and it produced anything it needed.

The passes were so large and distinct that it made counterfeiting them next to impossible. And the hall monitors like Mousey, or the students who sometimes filled in for her, could check them without having to get out of their chairs. Anything in the name of discipline.

The Tatler hall pass was a circular item created by the art class and had two finger holes on top that acted as a grip. But one of the other students was using it so Mr. Friedrich had to write one on a slip of paper for me. I was taking a walk on the wild side and Mousey knew it.

"Mr. Blazek, you don't seem to have a hall pass," Mousey slipped sideways out of her chair. It had a desk attached to the front of it so she could read a magazine while passing the time. All in all she had a pretty easy flop.

"You know me better than that." I smiled. After all, I was a senior and for three years she had been trying to nail me without any success. I was not a saint by any means but I did manage to stay one step ahead of her. And she knew it.

"Don't try to sweet talk me, Mr. Blazek. Just show me your pass or it's straight to Principal Tuck's office."

Her nose wrinkled and her eyes squinted. That's what I'd been waiting for. She figured just the mention of C. C. Tuck's name would drop me to my knees. But I was ready for her. It was the reason I took the long way to the chemistry classroom.

"Sure, Miss Dawson, here's my pass." I put my hand in my pants pocket and jiggled it around for a while, watching Mousey squirm. I knew she was hoping beyond hope that I would come out empty-handed. She was like a tigress waiting to pounce on an innocent lamb.

Finally, I handed her the piece of paper with Mr. Friedrich's signature on it.

"Coming from *The Tatler* I see." She examined it closely. "Where's your regular hall pass?"

"Maria, our gossip columnist, is using it. Any hot tips?"

"Not for publication." She actually smiled. "Now go on your way and don't dilly-dally."

"Yes ma'am," I headed toward the northeast stairway. Notch another one up for the kid.

West Tech had a lot of stairs. There was one stairwell in each corner of the building, plus the main one that Mousey patrolled that was at the front entrance. But that was a one-way stairway, down only, I guess because it went directly into the basement cafeteria. It was also the only one that went from the third to the fourth floor. Up there it went both ways. The corner stairs also went down into the basement. And we had an elevator and a sub-basement and some little rooms above the fourth floor and who knows what else.

Confusing? Yes, especially for the new students. But

everything at West Tech was done for a reason and it all made sense after a while.

I'm telling you this just to give you some idea of West Tech's total capacity. Attendance peaked at around 5000 students in the 1930s. It had more residents than some cities in Kansas. There were seniors who in three years had not seen half the building. You know how you fall into your own little ruts? That's what I'm talking about.

Each third floor chemistry class had a lab room attached to it. Sometimes you sat in the lab, sometimes you sat in the regular classrooms. I know because I was a chemistry major.

At West Tech every student had to declare a major like woodworking, foundry, electrical, welding or auto shop. Most were not geared for higher education so if you hoped to attend college you majored in chemistry. Like I explained before, college was pretty much out of my reach. No way could my parents afford to send me to the local university. Instead, after graduation, I was expected to find a job and help my family. But what the hell, I could dream, couldn't I?

I looked in Mr. Fleming's classroom and he was busy teaching ninth period. Damn. That meant that I'd have to wait until after school to interview him which meant that I'd be doing Tatler stuff on my own time. I hated that. My time was too valuable.

"They should pay me for this," I grumbled to myself.

I took a seat in the empty lab room next to Mr. Fleming's class. I had about a fifteen minute wait. There was no reading material lying around so my eyes began to wander.

It was a typical chemistry lab. The Periodic Table of Elements was up on the wall. There were a few posters showing high school students peering through microscopes. Bunsen burners were scattered around the tables.

I noticed some papers sitting on the teacher's desk. At first I was afraid to look at them. Maybe they were test questions and I'd be busted for good with that little slip. Mousey would love that. But Mr. Fleming was teaching a first year chemistry class and I was taking second year.

You know how it is, first you're scared, then you're curious. Maybe these were the famous experiments that he was working on. I had a guaranteed ten more minutes. Another thing about Dear Old West Tech, no one ever let you out of class early. Too much chaos.

I started looking through the papers, carefully keeping them in order. I could not make a whole lot of sense out of them because they were written in German. I knew German was supposed to be the language of science but it seemed a bit peculiar to me. I did not know Mr. Fleming was fluent in German. I was not even sure if he was of German descent.

The written text was punctuated with chemical formulas. All the calculations used the metric system, liters and grams, not pounds and ounces. Metrics were the also the basis of the scientific community but I had trouble converting them.

As a chemistry major I knew some of the chemist's language. I knew an acid from a base and understood the different symbols from The Periodic Table of Elements.

But I could not make heads or tails out of Mr. Fleming's calculations. They wouldn't help me much with the interview. No wonder he felt okay leaving them on his desk. He knew no one at Tech would be able to decipher their meaning.

I put the papers back on the desk just as the bell rang. The hallway was instantly cluttered with teenage humanity. I weaved my way back to Mr. Fleming's classroom, standing by the doorway as a couple suck-ups stood around his desk peppering the honored professor with a few more questions.

Couldn't they do this during class time? is what I wanted to know. *Don't they realize I have a trolley to catch?*

When they saw me standing there they quickly exited. I was surprised. I didn't know *The Tatler* carried so much clout.

"Ready for the big game?" I asked Siegfried

Walsh as he brushed by me.

"My shoulder hurts a little but I'll be all right," he answered without breaking his stride. He was the center on Tech's football team, a big dumb offensive lineman, not the kind of kid to talk to the teacher after class. Maybe he was worried about a grade that might keep him off the team.

The other student just nodded. He looked familiar but with 4500 students even a guy with my newspaper contacts could not place him.

"Mr. Fleming, do you have a minute?" I asked him.

Harold Fleming was a tall, skinny, blond man who wore suits that did not quite fit him. His face was lean, almost gaunt, as if he was carrying the weight of the world on his shoulders. His deep blue eyes looked tired.

"What do you need, Mr. Blazek?" he replied formally. He remembered me from my Chemistry I class.

"You know I write for *The Tatler*. I was wondering if I could interview you about this *Cleveland Press* article?" I put it on his desk.

"Oh, that." He picked it up. "I was not too happy about that article."

"Something wrong with it?"

"No, but there is such a thing as national security, you know. We could be going to war before you know it."

"Then they shouldn't have written it?"

"Not without talking to me first. You notice there are no quotes from me in there. I would have been against them printing it."

"That's what we were hoping, that you might add some personal insight to the subject."

"Well, I am in a bit of a hurry," he handed me back *The Press* article. He wasn't being very cooperative.

"So am I," I followed him as he walked back to the lab room that I had just left. "Is there a better time to talk?"

"What do you want to know?"

"What exactly are you working on?" I asked him.

"I can't tell you."

"Why not?"

"Can't tell you."

"Because it is top secret or because I would not understand?"

"Both."

"What can you tell me? The students have a famous teacher in their midst. They'd like to know a little bit about you."

"Aren't you a sports writer?"

"Yes."

He picked up the papers I had peeked at off his desk and began unlocking a built-in wood cabinet with a large round skeleton key.

"You can tell them I predict the Carpenters will beat

Lakewood in the big game." As he put the papers inside the cabinet it seemed like he purposely blocked my view of it with his body.

"By the time this goes to press the game will be over. How about, how long have you been working on this project?"

"A long time." He turned from the cabinet, clearly irritated by my questions. But the more he avoided them the more determined I was to find out why. He had lit my journalistic fire.

"Will it be hard teaching school while working on a government project?"

"These are dangerous times, we all have to make sacrifices." He absent-mindedly put the cabinet key in the top drawer of his desk.

"Can I quote you on that?"

"I suppose, is that all?"

"That's not much, is there anything else that you can add to *The Press* story?"

He began putting on his coat and hat, then stopped a second as if a thought had crossed his mind. "Yes, I would not have had this opportunity without the cooperation of the West Tech faculty and administration."

"Great, that's the kind of stuff we need. Anything else?" Mr. Fleming looked me straight in the eye and said nothing. He turned off the classroom lights and closed the door. I followed him into the hallway.

"My compliments to Mr. Friedrich," he said and touched the brim of his fedora. Then he disappeared into the mass of students exiting the school.

There's more to this story than meets the eye, I thought as I hurried to catch the Lorain Avenue trolley. *Thank God I write sports.*

CHAPTER FOUR:
The Lakewood Game

We were standing at the trolley stop at Bunts and Hilliard Roads, right in front of Lakewood High School, shivering in the night air. I pulled up my collar to protect my neck and looked over at my best friend, halfback Ed Gorski.

"You all right, Stash?"

"I still can't believe we lost," he stamped his feet to stay warm. He was still wearing his crimson and gray road football uniform under his long winter jacket. His shoulder pads, helmet and spikes were stuffed into a pillowcase tucked between his ankles.

"I meant, are you warm enough?"

"I don't feel nothin'." He grunted.

I could tell he didn't want to talk so we waited for the trolley in silence. Ed had played a great game. He ran for two touchdowns and intercepted a pass on defense. But Lakewood was too tough and beat Tech 14-12 because we could not make the points after the touchdowns.

Most of the rest of the team and the fans had

caught earlier trolleys back to the city but we stopped to visit Ed's aunt after the game. It was getting late and we were both tired.

The loss to suburban Lakewood, our historic rivals, was devastating. But they were a non-conference team that we always played the last game of the year. We were still on top in our division, the city of Cleveland's West Senate. That meant we had a ticket to the traditional championship game against the East Senate champs in Cleveland Stadium come Thanksgiving Day.

"I hope we didn't miss the last trolley," I said.

"They run all night on the weekends," he reminded me.

As I said "oh yeah" my eyes caught a solitary figure crossing the street toward us. The streetlight illuminated a female student carrying an instrument case. The falling snow framed her light green wool jacket. She was still wearing her red and white marching band boots.

"Hello, Eddie." She smiled at Gorski. "Great game."

"Thanks Doris," Ed's mood improved considerably. "You know my friend Vic."

"Sure, *The Tatler* guy." She shook my hand. I knew that I'd met her before but I could not remember when.

"You're running late," I said.

"Stopped to visit a relative."

"Us too," Ed answered for both of us.

Finally the trolley arrived. It was a bit crowded for a Friday night, but nothing like the before or after school rush hour.

We let Doris on first. She found an empty seat near the back of the trolley where there was a seat placed sideways. By that I mean you sat with the back of your head against the window and your feet in the aisle as opposed to the rest of the seats that were stacked in a row like at church. Ed sat next to her. I grabbed the first seat next to the sideways seat so we could talk easier. There was already a middle-aged man sitting in my seat looking out the window. He was holding a metal lunch bucket on his lap. No doubt he was working the midnight shift somewhere, probably the steel mills or oil refineries in the Flats.

The trolley was noisy, there were a lot of conversations going on at the same time even that late at night. I tried to join in with Ed and Doris but soon gave up. Ed obviously had a thing for Doris. But I wasn't sure that Doris felt likewise.

"Your friend play football for Tech?" the guy sitting next to me asked after a while. His face was chiseled with lines that made him look older than he probably was. I guessed that he worked near the blast furnace in the steel mills and that the heat had left its mark on his face.

"You could tell by his uniform, huh?"

"Yeah, I went to Tech for a few years, then my dad

passed away and I had to take a job in the mills."

"Sorry about that."

"Nothing to be sorry about, it was his time. You guys win?"

"Naw, we lost a close one."

"Too bad."

"How do you like working in the mills?"

"I'm livin' in Lakewood, ain't I?" he said with pride. "Tuck still the principal?"

"Oh yeah, he'll be there forever."

"That's one tough son-of-a-bitch but he's good for you young boys, keeps you out of trouble."

"That's what they say."

"You a senior?"

"Yeah, graduate in June if Tuck don't mess with me."

"You want a job in the mills you come see me, Joe Baxter, Republic Steel. We hire all the Tech kids we can. You can thank Tuck for that."

He started to get up so I stood up to let him out. He was going to transfer to the Lorain Avenue trolley to the Flats.

"Same goes for your friend," Baxter patted Ed on the knee with a hand that was the size of a tennis racket. He then made his way to the exit.

"Who was that?" Ed asked. He was so busy talking to Doris that he completely missed our conversation.

"I'll tell you later. It's our stop, too. How about

you Doris?"

"Mine, too," she said.

The three of us jumped off the trolley and walked over toward the Lorain Avenue transfer stop. A westbound trolley was bearing down on us and Doris ran for it. We were going eastbound.

"See you in English, Doris," Ed said as she jumped on her trolley.

"Good night, boys," she smiled.

Stash and I waited for our trolley in silence. Finally I broke the ice.

"You're taking a fancy to Doris, aren't you?"

"She's pretty neat," Stash admitted.

"What instrument does she play?"

"A clarinet. She has to carry it with her just like I do," he held up his pillowcase with pride.

"So that's how she got those strong arms."

"How would you know?" He glared at me.

"Just kidding, ya big lug, just kidding."

CHAPTER FIVE:
The Cafeteria

Wednesday mornings were my favorite day of the week. That was when *The Tatler* came out. It was only four pages, basically a large piece of paper folded in half. But it was chock full of interesting information.

West Tech was blessed with so many extracurricular activities that there was never any problem finding subjects to write about, even for a weekly newspaper.

My story on the Lakewood game was under a banner headline all the way across the top of page four, the Sports Page. For most of the guys that was the first place they looked. Everyone knew that Ed Gorski was my friend so I tried not to play him up too much, but it wasn't easy. The whole team revolved around him.

My story about Mr. Fleming was only a few paragraphs on the bottom of page three, our Features Page. It didn't even carry my byline. He didn't give me much to write about but I didn't care. I only did it to keep Mr. Friedrich happy.

The Tatlers were passed out during homeroom. By my fifth period lunch break most everyone would have had a chance to read it. I knew entering the cafeteria that I would hear about it. Especially from the football players. Most of them sat together.

The cafeteria at West Tech was as huge as everything else in the structure. It filled up most of the basement. But the food was good, almost like home cooking. There were no processed foods for our generation. Ethnic women cooked the same wholesome meals for us that they served their kids at home, only in larger quantities.

As I walked down the stairs to the cafeteria I kept my eyes peeled for football players. You never knew how they would react to my stories. They hadn't kicked my butt yet but there was always a first time.

I entered the cafeteria and jumped in the first available line. I cast a glance at the football team's fifth period table and they didn't notice me. (Lunch was served fourth, fifth and sixth periods.) That was a good sign, at least they were not gunning for me.

As I perused my choices of stuffed cabbage, meatloaf, or Swiss steak I heard a loud voice right behind me.

"Nice story, Blazek, after two years you're finally doing it right," Bruce Kwan, one of the team's ends, spoke out. He was talking around a pair of female students that were between us. And he was standing in line with Siegfried Walsh, another lineman. Both guys played offense and defense.

Since his attitude was complimentary I let the coeds go in front of me. If he had been belligerent I would have used them as a buffer and disappeared into the crowd.

"Thanks," I said.

"I don't know, I didn't like him telling everyone about Fleming's project," Walsh said.

"What are you talking about?" Kwan asked Walsh.

"His story about Mr. Fleming," Walsh said as we moved through the line. Middle-aged ladies wearing hairnets and aprons plopped meat, mashed potatoes and vegetables on our trays like mess sergeants in the army. "I thought it stunk."

"I'm talking about the Lakewood game," Kwan said to Walsh as we approached the cashier. "Nice job, Victor. Want to sit with the team?"

"I would but there's a certain girl I want to talk to," I gave the cashier a dime for my meal.

"What's wrong, can't hang out with the team without your buddy Gorski?" Walsh was acting tough, trying to cover up his mix-up about *The Tatler* stories. I wondered how he knew that I wrote the Fleming story. Then I remembered seeing him talking to Mr. Fleming after chemistry class, right before I interviewed him.

"I'll sit with the team when you learn how to hike," I said. His two bad snaps cost us the extra points that lost the Lakewood game. I played it down in my story but now I wish I hadn't.

"At least I made the team, sissy." Walsh dropped his tray on the conveyer without paying for it and walked up to me, glaring in my face, looking for a fight.

"Hey, take it outside," Kwan said. "You want to get suspended?"

"Anytime, anyplace," I told Walsh even though I didn't mean it. He was twice my size and had arms larger than my thighs.

"You're on," Walsh hollered as I turned my back on them.

I started looking for a girl to sit with. Any girl. Luckily, Maria from *The Tatler* was sitting at the end of a long wooden table picking at her lunch as if she was lost in thought.

"Where's all your friends?" I asked her. She had long dark hair, curled like Betty Grable's. She was wearing a plaid skirt and a white blouse that was the style then.

"I'm waiting for Olga," she said. 'Nice story."

"I liked your bit on Mrs. Caruso. I didn't know she was engaged to Mr. Dvorak?"

"That's my job, to sniff out the juicy gossip inside these brick walls." She laughed.

"What do you know about Doris Fidelmeister?"

"What do you mean?" I could tell her interest was aroused.

"My friend Ed Gorski ran into her after the Lakewood game. I could tell he liked her."

"Doris is a beautiful flower waiting to be picked, but by the right guy."

"I don't get you."

"She's a hot tomato, you dummy. She's smart, she's pretty and she plays a mean clarinet, but I don't think she likes Ed that way."

"What way?"

"You know, boyfriend, girlfriend way. Do I have to spell everything out for you?"

"I know how to spell."

"You boys are so dense." She went back to moving her corn around with her fork.

"So who does she like?"

"Uh-oh. Do I smell a little rivalry here?" She stopped eating again and looked me right in the eye.

"Nothing for publication. But you said she's a hot tomato."

"Well, so am I. How come you never ask about me?"

"You? You're my *Tatler* buddy. Wouldn't that be a conflict of interest?"

Just then Maria's girl friend, Olga, dropped her tray across the table from us.

"Men," Maria said.

"What?" Olga asked.

"I was just leaving for the noon movie," I said. "Nice seeing you, Olga. See you ninth period." I said to Maria.

"You should be so lucky."

I skipped away in a hurry. The way it was with Maria was like this. I liked her. I liked her a lot. She was my favorite person at *The Tatler*. I would've liked to take her to the Lyceum Theatre for a Saturday matinee. But you know how guys worry about silly things at that age. Dating Maria would be like an office romance in the real world. What do I say to her when we're working on *The Tatler* Monday afternoon? Especially if I tried something stupid like holding her hand. I had to let that hot tomato ripen on the vine.

After hearing what Maria had to say about Doris I decided to try to "accidently" run into her. But where to find her? I thought she had the same fifth period lunch that I did but I seldom saw her there. It was a big school but once you were crammed together inside the cafeteria you usually recognized everyone.

At Tech there were a couple of lunch options, once again due to its size. First of all, the forty-minute lunch period was split in half. You ate either the first or second twenty minute half, then moved out of the way to make room for the next wave of hungry students.

What you did with your free half was up to you. One option was what we called "the noon movies" even though they were shown six times a day. For two cents a day you bought a ticket in the basement ticket booth and went to see a movie in the auditorium.

They were feature-length movies but they were

shown like soap operas, in twenty-minute segments. You had to hurry from the cafeteria to the auditorium or you'd miss the beginning of each segment. Tech was run like a well-oiled machine. Keeping the students on a short leash kept them out of trouble.

Another option was to go dancing at the "Rec Room," short for recreation room. Dancing was more popular back then. The big band era was in full swing and everyone was hip to the sound.

The Rec Room was in the corner of the basement. It wasn't very large considering its popularity but, once again, it was probably planned that way. A small Victrola in the corner spun 78 rpm records. There was room for maybe ten couples to swing while the gawkers stood against the walls. It was not unusual for the girls to dance with each other since a lot of guys were too shy to embarrass themselves in front of the crowd. Twenty minutes was only long enough for a couple dances but it kept the students busy and blew off some steam for the rest of the day.

The guys who were good dancers were much sought after by the ladies. I, on the other hand, was more of a wallflower so I usually opted for the noon movie, unless it was a stinker. We were in the middle of *Test Pilot* starring Clark Gable and Myrna Loy. Everyone was trying to see it because it featured scenes from the Cleveland National Air Races that we had watched over Labor

Day. But I had never seen Doris there so I thought I'd try the Rec Room.

It was a long shot. If I didn't see her in the cafeteria the chances were slim that she'd be in the Rec Room. Maybe she ate the second half of fifth period, but for some reason I remembered seeing her the first half earlier in the year.

So I wandered over to the Rec Room, following the sounds of Glen Miller's band wafting through the hallway. As I made my way through the crowd watching the dancers I realized that although I knew a large number of students at Tech I only had a few real friends.

I shook a lot of hands and smiled a few hellos like a politician but I didn't feel real comfortable stopping to speak with anyone. I saw a few girls who knew Doris but didn't want to give away my intentions.

Hmm, what to do next? I had given up a key segment of *Test Pilot* and had nothing to show for it. And old Clark Gable was just beginning to test the military planes that really wowed the students. Instead I was watching the hep cats cut a rug. Time was running out.

Then it hit me. There was a third lunch option I forgot about because I never considered it. The library. Some students went to the library before or after lunch to catch up on their homework. Maybe that's where Doris was hiding.

I only had a few minutes to make my move but was

unsure as how to proceed. It was too late to go to the library. At Tech you had five minutes between periods to make your move and that was it. Once you moved from point A to point B you were committed until the bell rang. There was no wandering around the hallways. After visiting the Rec Room I was stuck there.

Or was I? The library was on the third floor in the middle of the building, right in the heart of Mousey's territory. But I had kept my paper pass from Mr. Friedrich in my wallet for just such an emergency.

My heart was thumping. Did I dare risk the wrath of Mousey and C. C. Tuck just on the chance that Doris would be in the library for a few minutes?

What the hell? You only live once. My emotions were taking over for my brain. Before I knew it I whipped out my pen and changed the date and period on my hall pass. Mr. Friedrich, please forgive me.

I walked up the main "down only" stairway from the basement very slowly, stopping to catch my breath before I hit the first floor. I tried to keep my composure as I peeked around the corner toward Mousey's chair. And miracle of miracles, she was nowhere to be seen. She must have taken a break to the lady's room or something.

Oh lucky day. I put it in second gear and raced up the steps to the library. When I opened the library door five minutes before the end of the period every student inside looked up at me. Oops, I did not count on that.

"May I help you, Victor?" the librarian immediately confronted me with an icy manner. Fortunately, I had logged enough time in those book-lined shelves that she knew me by name.

"Sorry, Mrs. Kirk," I whispered. "I need a quick fact for *The Tatler* and I only have a few minutes between classes."

"In that case, can I be of assistance?" she smiled at me and gave a look to the rest of the students that said go back to your studies.

Mrs. Kirk was a terribly skinny lady that a good gust of wind could blow away. Her gray hair was in a bun on her head but she liked to wear flashy dresses and high heels like a Broadway actress. The rumor was that she once performed in Vaudeville.

"No thank you, I know what I need."

I smiled back at her and turned to survey the landscape. You are no doubt tired of hearing it but the library was also quite a big area, taking a large chunk out of the third floor. It held more books than some of the branches of the Cleveland Public Library. I could see only about a third of it from the main desk and Doris was nowhere to be found.

I slowly walked along the walls surveying the hardcover books like I knew what I was doing. I could feel Mrs. Kirk's eyes drilling into the back of my head.

As I pretended to search the shelves I looked out of

the corner of my eyes for Doris. I turned one corner, then another, leaving Mrs. Kirk behind. I was just about to give up when it happened.

There was Doris, head bent over a thick textbook, writing on a sheet of notebook paper. My heart began to race again. I slowly grabbed the first book I could find off the shelf and moved in her direction.

I quietly sat in the seat next to her, acting as if I was so absorbed in my own book that I did not notice her. She looked up and smiled as I sat down. I looked up from my book and smiled back. We were both too afraid to say anything. We both looked back down at our books.

Then the bell rang and everyone stood up and started talking, including us.

"Doris, what are you doing here?"

"Catching up on my homework, and you?"

"Just a little research for the *The Tatler*."

Around the World in 80 Days by Jules Verne? What kind of story are you working on?"

"It's a long story." I was speechless. I hadn't looked at the title when I grabbed it off the shelf.

"I read your Lakewood game story," she said as she picked up her notebook. "Nice job."

"Thanks," I stammered.

"Well, nice seeing you." She began to leave.

"Where's your next class?" I didn't want to let her go

after all the trouble I went to finding her.

"Steno, room 236, and you?"

"English, 204," I followed her out of the library. "Do you always go to the library during lunch?"

"Yeah, I have to do my homework. I work after school."

"Oh yeah, where at?"

"The Western Manufacturing Company on Clark Avenue, I'm the receptionist."

"I go right by there on my way home," I lied.

"You should stop and see me sometime."

"The boss don't care?"

"As long as you don't stay too long," she winked. I instantly knew I'd be visiting her the first chance I could, even though it was out of my way.

"Great, see you at work." By this time we had walked down the steps together and had to split for different corridors on the second floor.

"Bye-bye, Victor." She departed with a sweet little wave of her hand. I could hardly wait to see her again.

CHAPTER SIX:
The Charity Game

The West Tech Carpenters were the champs of the West Senate football conference. Their reward was to play the East Senate's Cathedral Latin Lions for the city championship in the annual Charity Game.

It was called The Charity Game because Cleveland's morning newspaper, *The Plain Dealer*, used the great interest in high school sports to raise money for its "Give-A-Christmas Fund." It helped the city's poor people enjoy the Holiday Season.

The Charity Game originated in 1931 during the depths of the Great Depression. It was played on Thanksgiving Day at Cleveland's downtown Stadium, the same place the professional Cleveland Rams football team and Cleveland Indians baseball team played.

Cleveland Stadium was a huge sports edifice. There was room for over 80,000 fans. And thanks to intense media coverage by the city's three daily newspapers the Charity Game would attract over 40,000 fans at a time the Rams were only pulling in 20,000.

Not only did the top two football teams in the city play

for bragging rights, the half-time show featured marching bands from both conferences. This was a brilliant marketing ploy that helped boost attendance. For every kid on the field there was usually a family full of fans in the stands.

Many of Tech's 4500 student base and their families planned to view the game Thanksgiving morning before partaking in the usual holiday festivities. Ed Gorski was playing on the football team. Doris was marching in the band. And I was covering the game for *The West Tech Tatler* AND *The Cleveland News*.

The News was giving the sports editors of the two high school team's newspapers space for their own view of the game. And paying us ten bucks each. It was my first professional gig.

I was excited as hell and looking for a way to scoop the competition. Not just my Cathedral Latin brother but also the big boys from the *Cleveland Press*, *Plain Dealer* and *News*. So I talked Tech's football coach, Stan Schwartz, into letting me ride to the game on the team bus and hang with the guys before and after the game.

Usually I covered the game from the stands at West Tech's field. This time I was hoping for an inside story. I would show the game from the player's view, especially what it was like for a high school kid to play in Cleveland Stadium in front of 40,000 screaming fans. Talk about a pressure cooker.

On top of that I was supposed to take some action

photos for *The Tatler*. Our staff photographer, Jack Norris, had to go out of town with his family for the holiday so Mr. Friedrich dumped the job on me. Especially since I already had access to the field.

Jack showed me how to use the camera but it was an awesome responsibility. The Graphlex 4x5 inch format was a pro camera that was used commercially. It was the only camera the school owned. It was used for *The Tatler* and yearbook pictures. All the photography majors had to buy their own cameras for the class and since it was still the tail end of the Depression most of them were poor substitutes for the Graphlex.

So at 8 a.m. on Thanksgiving morning, November 29, 1941, I was waiting at West Tech's football field for the players to finish dressing in the locker room. They weren't allowed to use the Rams locker room so they had to put on their football uniforms before jumping on the team bus.

Taking a team bus was as much of a treat for the players as it was for me. Normally the players had to find their own transportation to away games. Fortunately, West Tech's football field was the premier facility in the city so most of our games were played at home where the Carpenters could use their own lockers.

And not only did the football team have its own bus for the Charity Game, so did the marching band. As I waited outside the school on the cold fall morning two buses pulled into the school parking lot between the school and the football field.

Then I heard a whooping and a hollering louder than at any game I'd ever attended. At first I thought the football team was really psyched up for this gig. But it turned out to be the marching band running out of the school's northwest entrance, the one below *The Tatler* office, toward their bus.

They had changed into their band uniforms and were carrying their instrument cases. School spirit was oozing out of their pores. I walked over to the bus, hoping to catch Doris' eye. I had not yet been able to visit her after-school job.

She was blabbing with her friend, Lois Berger, the trombone player, and did not see me standing nearby. I intercepted her just as she was about to step up on the bus.

"Good luck," I said.

"Victor, what are you doing here?" she asked, letting Lois go in front of her.

"I'm riding on the football team's bus."

"Swell. Are you excited?"

"I am now. They're letting me go on the field. And I'm taking pictures for *The Tatler*."

I held up the Graphlex camera. Doris looked impressed.

"I'll look for you," she said.

"Me, too. I'll try to take your picture."

Mr. Maricic, the band director, came up behind us. "Let's go Doris. Today's the big day."

"Yes sir," she said.

I took her elbow and helped her up the steps. It was the first time I had touched her and a tingle went through my body. She fumbled trying to make her clarinet case fit through the doorway so I took it from her hands and handed it to her when she was inside.

"Break a leg," I said. She smiled and quickly went to the back of the bus. She waved from the bus window as it took off for downtown. Something inside me clicked on and I suddenly realized she was the one. My life was somehow beginning to make sense.

The football team was coming out of the northeast door by the boy's gym. I ran over to meet the players.

"Hey Stash," I said to my man, Gorski. "How you feeling?"

"Scared," he muttered so his teammates would not hear him.

"You? Of what?"

"What if I mess up, fumble or something? I'm going to feel like a jerk."

"You'll do great, you're the big guy, once you get out there it'll all fall into place."

"I hope so." He shook his head.

Compared to the marching band the football team was subdued. They quietly took their seats on the bus.

These guys were already used to playing in front of big crowds. A regular Friday night at West Tech's field would draw 15,000 fans.

Still, this was the Big Game in the Big Stadium for all the marbles. Many of the players were seniors who for three years dreamed of playing in the Charity Game. It was the Super Bowl of high school sports and most of them shared Ed's foreboding. They were strictly business.

I looked at it as great material for my story. I figured once they stepped in front of the crowd all their fears would evaporate.

First, the bus dropped us off at a special entrance to the stadium, the same one the pros used to avoid the fans. Then we were shepherded into the bowels of the concrete structure. Then we had to wait around for the PA announcer to introduce the team.

The players reminded me of a bunch of horses before a big race. They were stomping their cleats instead of hooves, to ward off the cold and steady their nerves, chomping at the bit to bolt out of the gate. The anticipation was nerve wracking.

"Try not to look at the fans," I told Ed.

"Are you kidding? The first thing I'm doing is finding my mom and dad. They're sitting in the bleachers."

Finally, the PA announcer said, "Representing the West Senate Conference, the West Tech Carpenters."

"Let's go guys," Coach Schwartz said. "Give 'em hell."

Then it all happened so quickly. The crowd roared and we headed out onto the frozen field. It snowed the night before and there were piles of snow around the field perimeter but we ran right through them.

I was supposed to head to the bench while the team lined up at the 40-yard line, opposite the Latin team on the other 40-yard line. There was still so much snow on the field that the ground crew used coal dust to mark the yard lines.

I felt like an ant in a crystal ball. The stadium was huge and everyone was so far away. There were a million eyes watching our every move and I froze for a second, letting it all sink in.

What a day! First Doris and now this. Win or lose, I decided to enjoy the moment for all it was worth.

The football game was one of the most exciting in Charity Game history. The lead kept going back and forth. When Tech scored a touchdown the north side of the stadium would erupt in cheers since that was the side where the West Senate supporters sat. When Latin scored the south side cheered wildly for the same reason.

The star players in those days played both offense and defense. So by halftime Ed Gorski was beat but happy. He'd already scored a touchdown and recovered a fumble. The score was 12-12 and both teams seemed evenly matched.

"Great half, Stash," I said.

"So far, so good."

Coach Schwartz took the team inside the stadium to keep warm and make plans for the second half. I wanted to go with them and hear the coach's comments but finding Doris was more important.

The halftime show featured the bands from twenty-four area high schools. Despite the cold weather most of the 46,686 fans stayed in their seats to watch the bands form a huge V for victory sign. They also did a dot-dot-dash Morse code version of the letter V.

Even though the country was not yet at war most Americans could read the writing on the wall. Germany was attacking our British allies and before long we would have to help them. If not we risked fighting them on our own shores.

But war was the furthest thing from my mind that cold November afternoon. I was trying to spot Doris among the Carpenter marching band.

There were musicians moving in every direction. Planning the V routine was just as complicated as Coach Schwartz' game plan but the average football fan did not appreciate it.

The Tech band was between the Shaker Heights and Parma High bands on the opposite side of the field. The musicians stood three abreast to form the thickness of the letter. Our school's uniforms included white hats that helped keep them warm but made it hard to distinguish individuals.

I looked and looked but I could not find Doris. I wanted to take a picture of her in all her glory. I had already taken a few of my buddy Gorski.

Finally, I decided to run over to the other side of the field. The halftime show was winding down and time was running out. I had to go around the end zone to keep from interfering with the band program. By the time I made it to the Cathedral Latin side of the field the bands were filing back into the stadium.

I found Tech's band and found Doris. She was still marching and playing the clarinet, right behind her friend Lois' trombone. I snuck up as close as I could and snapped a photo. Then I flipped over the film plate and snapped another one. The camera did not have automatic lenses like they have today. After each photo you had to replace the film, adjust the light intake, change the shutter speed and plan your angle. I only carried a dozen film plates, each with two shots on them. If you were lucky you took twenty-four pictures a game and on half of them something would go wrong. So you tried to make each one a masterpiece.

Doris saw me take the first photo and then winked at me as I took the second one. I could feel it was a beauty. I gave her a wave and raced back around to the Tech side, just in time for the beginning of the second half.

The second half was just as exciting as the first half. The crowd was psyched like a pro playoff game today. Both sides were pumped up and played hard.

Latin took the second half kickoff and worked their way down to Tech's three yard line. Then Tech's defense stiffened. They put on one of the greatest goal line stands in Charity Game history. Latin tried a fourth down end around but Gorski stuffed their best runner for a two-yard loss. The Tech fans erupted.

Then Tech turned the tables and drove all the way back down to Latin's goal line. This time Latin did their own goal line stand. Now the fans on both sides of the stadium were going crazy. The sound was bouncing off the walls.

And so it went the entire second half. Both teams moved the ball well but neither could cross the goal line. I began to wonder what would happen if they tied. Would there be an overtime period to declare a winner or would they just call the season a tie?

I wondered why I had not thought of that before the game. But I was pretty sure that the officials had planned for it. The players on both teams began to look tired. It was tough playing both offense and defense as many of them did for the entire game.

Finally with less than two minutes left on the clock both coaches seemed desperate for a break. It came but in the strangest fashion.

Tech had driven to Latin's twenty yard line. They were running out of time and Latin's defense stiffened once again. Coach Schwartz did not have much confidence in his kicker, William "Crazy Legs" Archibald. He was a converted soccer player from Manchester, England.

But like most of the fans in the stands he could not stomach a tie in such an important game. He would later explain to me for my News story that he figured the worst that could happen would be for "Crazy Legs" to miss and Latin would take the ball at the twenty.

Coach Schwartz thought that Tech's defense could surely hold them for the last few minutes. In his wildest dreams he could not imagine Latin blocking the kick, picking it up and racing for the winning touchdown with less than a minute left in the game.

But that's what happened. Tech's fans watched in a state of shock. The game was over and so was their season. Our hopes for a city championship were crushed.

I took a few photos of the player's reactions. Later they would prove to be moving testimonies to the agony of defeat. But at the time I was just going through the motions.

The bus ride home was the toughest trip of my life. The entire team felt the same way. The whole school was in a state of shock. We felt our lives were practically over. What could happen to us that could possibly be worse?

CHAPTER SEVEN:
Pearl Harbor

In the days following Tech's heartbreaking loss in the Charity Game the entire school was in a massive funk. Nothing seemed to matter anymore. To young high school students like us it was a crushing blow. It was like breaking up with your girlfriend the day before she was crowned Homecoming Queen. Even Tech's faculty seemed to be just going through the motions until the Christmas break when there would be time to heal the emotional scars.

Then on Sunday, December 7, 1941, everything changed. It started off as a normal day around my home. In other words, the craziness began at sunrise. We lived in the downstairs half of a double home off Denison Avenue, a couple miles from West Tech. My parents rented the upstairs half to help pay for the mortgage.

I was the sixth of seven children. I had two older sisters, three older brothers and a younger sister, all West Tech alumni. My oldest brother, William, died a few years earlier, drowning in the neighborhood swimming pool. My mother was still shook up from that tragedy.

Another brother, Johnny, contracted polio when he was young and wore metal braces on his legs. He studied engineering at Fenn College downtown and still lived at home. My oldest sister, Olga, was already married and had a baby but she was a frequent visitor while her husband Elmer worked at the Sohio Oil Refinery in the Flats.

My other sister, Eva, worked at the May Company department store downtown. She also still lived at home. It was hard for a girl to make enough money to support herself right out of high school. Back in those days a lady pretty much had to hook up with a man before she could go out into the real world.

My other brother, Andy, was already in the army. He was stationed in Alaska in case we were invaded by the Russians, who were supposed to be our allies. America did not trust their leader, Joseph Stalin, and neither did we, even though we were of Russian descent. In fact, my father hated him with a passion. He hated him worse than Adolph Hitler.

My youngest sister, Anna, was a sophomore at Tech. Since she was a girl and two years younger than me we didn't associate much at school.

We only had two bedrooms and they didn't even have doors, just drapes across a pole like shower curtains. And since one of the bedrooms was reserved for mom and pop, you can imagine the bizarre sleeping arrangements for us kids. The girls slept in a double bed in the other bedroom. Us guys shared a couch and the floor. It was every man for himself come lights-out time.

Despite the cramped environment, the household ran pretty smoothly during the week. My father worked nights at the railroad and slept days so we did not see much of him. The rest of us were busy with school or work.

The house did have a large kitchen and dining room. This was my mother Mary's domain. There was always a big pot of chicken soup or beef stew and a loaf of home-made bread to keep our bellies full despite our different schedules.

But on Sundays the whole family took the trolley to church at the St. Theodosius Russian Orthodox Cathedral. My father was one of the church's founding members. He helped build it when he first came over from the old country.

St. Theodosius sits on the edge of Cleveland's Flats area. You could stroll behind the church, visit the graves in the cemetery and look out on a fabulous site. The Flats are the area along the Cuyahoga River where all the city's heavy industry was. There were steel mills, oil refineries, railroads, piles of coal and sand, all the raw materials that were needed to keep America's economy up and running. You name it and you could find it there. My brother-in-law Elmer called it "The Industrial Might of Mid-America."

Our usual Sunday routine was to return home from church in the afternoon so my mother could put out a big spread. Then we would all sit around the dining room table for a family meal together.

After church on December 7, 1941, my dad headed straight to the bedroom for an afternoon nap before dinner. It kept him in his normal workday routine.

My brother Johnny was sitting on the couch in our small living room resting his braced legs on the coffee table. He was listening to the New York Philharmonic Society orchestra on the RCA radio in the corner. Johnny was the only one with any culture in our family. Because of his disease he was forced to spend a lot more time indoors than the rest of us. So he read a lot of books and listened to different kinds of music. I couldn't understand what he liked about that classical stuff. I was more into the swing music of the times. The big band sounds.

But I liked sitting next to him, keeping him company. You could learn a lot in a few minutes visiting with my brother Johnny, if you took the time. A lot of people shied away from him because of his braces, which was a pity because they missed a lot.

The girls were helping my mother in the kitchen.

I was still feeling depressed about Tech's big football loss, but it seemed petty compared to my brother's handicap.

It was bitter cold outside so we were stuck indoors. We could smell the aroma of stuffed cabbages, homemade dumplings and fresh baked bread. The family tradition was not to eat lunch after church so we would be hungry for the big dinner. Our taste buds were drooling while we made small talk.

I was asking Johnny about college. How tough were his engineering courses? How different was it from West Tech? He was telling me how being a Tech graduate gave him a leg up on most of his peers. As a chemistry major at Tech he had taken college level chemistry, physics, and math while still in high school.

Olga's three-year-old son, Jeff, had just jumped on the couch with us. Olga asked us to watch him while she helped our mom in the kitchen. Elmer had stayed at their apartment to catch up on some rest after working double shifts all week. The only good thing about the coming war was that it was cranking up the economy.

"Hey Uncle Johnny," he said, running around the coffee table, holding onto his leg braces. He was just beginning to learn how to talk and could already speak better English than our parents.

"Leave those alone, Jeffrey," I scolded him.

"Oh, it's okay, Victor," Johnny said. "He can't hurt them, they don't have much feeling."

"You want a horsy ride," I offered Jeffrey as I got down on my knees. He used the coffee table as a launching pad, jumped on my back, and knocked me flat on the floor.

Johnny let out a hearty laugh. I grabbed Jeffrey, put him in a wrestling hold and began tickling him.

Then it happened.

"We interrupt this program for an important announcement."

Jeffrey was squealing like a stuffed pig so I tried to quiet him down.

"The Japanese have attacked the United States Pearl Harbor naval base in Hawaii. Much of our Pacific Fleet has been destroyed by Japanese bombers. President Roosevelt is going to ask Congress for a Declaration of War tomorrow."

I shook the three-year-old off my back. He started crying as I ran into the kitchen to bring everyone into the living room. Johnny pulled his legs off the coffee table and bent his head closer to the radio. My sisters started crying louder than Jeffery.

My mother kept asking, "What is this, what is this?" changing from English to Russian back to English again. By the time the announcer filled in the details our whole family looked at each other in a state of shock.

"What does this mean?" my mother asked me in her broken English, tears in her eyes because everyone else was crying. She did not understand, but feared the worst.

Suddenly my father appeared from the bedroom. He stuck his pipe in his mouth and lit it. "Dees eez not good," he told her and then he put his arm around her waist. It was one of the few times I ever saw him show her a sign of affection.

My father spoke the least English of any of us. He had fought in the Russian-Turkish war. They had a much cruder draft method in the old country. The Army just came into his village and took away all the young men. Many of them never returned.

He came to America to escape the Russian government's oppression. But now his sons were going to have to defend his adopted country.

CHAPTER EIGHT:
Tuck Takes Charge

It was Monday morning and we were at war. On the trolley ride to Tech it was quieter than normal. Even the usual collection of public transit weirdos kept to themselves. The strange bearded guy who usually rocked back and forth in his seat like a baby seemed in a daze, barely moving his huge frame. The smelly woman we called "the klepto lady" was actually reading the morning *Plain Dealer* for a change. The word on the street was that she spent her days shoplifting at the big department stores downtown. I never saw her read a paper before.

Even the rowdy kids and third shift working stiffs on their way home were in a somber mood, trying to grasp the seriousness of the situation. What would the Japanese attack on Pearl Harbor mean to them? How would it affect their families, their jobs, their futures? No one seemed to know yet.

At West Tech 4500 of us walked into the school without the usual horseplay, cussing and cajoling. Our morning enthusiasm was dampened by a quiet anticipation. How would the grand old school react to the new world order? Only time would tell.

Homeroom was between first and second periods because some students would do work-study programs early in the morning or do phys-ed outside the school like the swimming classes at the Clark Recreation Center.

My homeroom was in the basic mechanics room of the basement. As soon as I walked in our teacher, Mr. Bader, cornered me. "I need you to take this note to the office, pronto," he said. "Make sure you give it to Assistant Principal Jameson. And be back by announcements."

"No problem, sir," I answered sharply. I feigned a salute to Mr. Bader. I was preparing for my military career but he did not see the humor in it. Although Mr. Bader was one of Tech's youngest and most popular teachers, sometimes he got a bug up his butt. Like when we called him a "camel jockey" because of his Lebanese descent. Everyone had their limits and you had to know them if you wanted to survive at Tech.

Since I was a few minutes early for homeroom I had plenty of time to make the trip. The announcements usually came over the PA a few minutes after the bell rang, giving the teacher just enough time to take attendance.

But when I entered the main office everything was

in an uproar. The school secretaries, who usually sat behind the main counter, were all up on their feet running hither and yon.

"I have a note for Mr. Jameson from Mr. Bader," I hollered at Miss Smith above the din. She was the student's main contact with the administration.

"I'll see that he gets it," she held out her hand as she walked by, barely slowing her pace.

I pulled the note back to my chest, stopping her in her tracks. "Mr. Bader said I should give it to Mr. Jameson myself."

Miss Smith had a look on her face I had never seen before in the three years I had known her. She wasn't used to students talking back to her.

"He said it was important," I added. Miss Smith sensed that it must be serious enough to respect Mr. Bader's wishes. And she was in a hurry.

"Stay right there," she said.

I almost told her I was supposed to be back in homeroom for the morning announcements but decided it was more important to deliver my message. A few other students stopped by delivering paperwork and a couple teachers stopped in to check their mailboxes. They were on the wall opposite the counter.

Then Maria stopped by.

"What are you doing here?" she asked me.

"Waiting to see Mr. Jameson, and you?"

"I read the PA announcements. Are you in trouble?" Mr. Jameson was in charge of discipline for the boys.

"With Mr. Jameson? No. I have a message for him. Where do you read the announcements?"

"The radio room's right back here. Want to listen?"

"Is that all right?"

"Sure, but you have to be real quiet."

I had always wondered where the strange voices that came over the school during homeroom originated. And I had forgot that Maria was one of those voices. So I followed her to a room behind the office. I figured that Miss Smith would find me eventually.

"Maria, you're late, and who's that?" Mr. Kovach practically screamed at her. He was the teacher in charge of the PA announcements.

"You know Mr. Blazek. He writes for *The Tatler*." She pointed at a chair for me to sit in. "He wants to do a story about us for *The Argosy*." *The Argosy* was Tech's literary magazine.

"I don't care who he is, this is not a good day," Mr. Kovach said. "Sorry, sonny," he said to me, "but you'll have to leave."

"Sure. See ya, Maria." I stood back up before my butt actually hit the bottom of the chair. But just as I turned to leave Mr. Jameson walked in.

"Here's your copy," he handed Mr. Kovach a pile of blue papers almost like blueprints. "Mr. Tuck will be here in a few minutes."

Suddenly the whole room went quiet. I froze in my tracks. Just the mention of Tuck's name had that effect on the school. Then Mr. Jameson noticed me. "What do you have for me, Victor?"

I handed him Mr. Bader's note and began to leave the room. Mr. Jameson read it quickly, shook his head, cleared his throat and pointed me back to my seat. He tried to say something but could not. "Stay put," he muttered.

It was 9:12 a.m., time for the morning announcements. 4500 students and 200 teachers were sitting quietly in 200 rooms scattered around the massive building waiting for their instructions from headquarters.

"BONG, BONG, BONG." Pat O'Leary hit a strange instrument called "The Bells" that was actually a mini-xylophone. He was the lead man in all the student plays, Tech's top thespian. Then he took his place behind George Duebel and Maria Monticelli. They were all veteran actors from the West Tech stage.

The three students stood in a line behind the microphone. It was the stand-up kind, attached to a large pole on a round stand, like the ones you see in movies about old time radio shows. Mr. Kovach handed each announcer a stack of blue papers. They took turns stepping up to the mike, reading their shtick, then returning to the back of the line. There were no rehearsals. This was live radio.

George went first. "Good Morning West Tech, here are your announcements for today, Monday, December 8, 1941."

Maria was next. "The lunch specials today are fried perch with French fries and spaghetti and meatballs, coleslaw is optional."

Then it was Pat's turn. "There will be a special meeting of the student government's General Organization during eighth period today. All student representatives will be excused from their classes to attend."

"The Chess Club meets after school during tenth period today in room 212. New members are welcome," George said.

"The Amateur Radio Club will meet tenth period Thursday in the fourth floor radio room," Maria announced. "Mr. Fleming reports that they will be making plans for their annual trip, so attendance is required."

Maria looked up as Mr. Jameson quietly entered the room again. The students continued their announcements about Tech's many extra-curricular activities while he took the bottom page from Mr. Kovach's pile and wrote a few notes on it. The final page fell to Pat O'Leary.

"There will be a new noon movie starting today. *Sergeant York*, starring Gary Cooper." Then Pat paused a second as he read Mr. Jameson's scribbled notes. And he coughed. Pat O'Leary never coughed, it was very unprofessional of him but he had to clear his throat. "And now a few words from our Principal, Mr. Tuck."

And exactly on cue Cecil Charles "C. C." Tuck walked through the radio room door, so much bigger than life that he had to bow his head a bit to fit through the doorway. I automatically stood up from my chair. The three PA students cautiously stepped back from the microphone in unison.

I could not recall C.C. Tuck making a PA announcement before. Although he could be seen everywhere, roaming the halls and the streets around the school looking for truants, he kept his contact with the students to a minimum so that when he did speak you listened and you listened good if you knew what was good for you.

C.C. Tuck was huge man by 1940 standards. He was six foot four inches in height when students five foot ten were considered tall. For example, Tech's football team's offensive line only averaged 150 pounds and they were considered among the toughest in the area. And he had already been Tech's principal forever. The school was molded in his image and he ruled it with an iron hand.

He had a rugged face, a square jaw and piercing blue eyes. He had played football for Knute Rockne at Notre Dame and worked his way through college as a semi-pro boxer. That's why he had a reputation for being as tough as nails.

As Tuck stepped up to the microphone Mr. Kovach struggled with the pole, trying to loosen the nut between its two sections so he could extend it upwards. Tuck brushed him aside with a sweep of his arm and picked up the mike with his two large hands like it was a portable microphone. He held it close to his mouth and turned to look at us. It seemed like he needed an audience. I could imagine the kids in my homeroom sitting on the edges of their seats, waiting for his words, like the voice of God coming out of a little box by the ceiling in room 86.

"My fellow faculty and students," he began slowly. He wasn't reading from a script, he was talking from his heart. "As you know our country was attacked yesterday and today President Roosevelt is going to ask Congress for a Declaration of War against Japan. Germany will probably be next. The days ahead are going to be hard. Our country is going to have to make many sacrifices. And West Tech is going to do its part to help win this war. We will collect rubber to make jeep tires and we will collect the leftover fat from our dinners to make explosives and we will collect tin cans to turn into bullets."

He paused and looked me right in the eye. "We will all do our part," he repeated for emphasis. "I have contacted the War Department and pledged that our school is going to raise money to help the

Air Force buy a B-17 bomber." His voice began to rise and his gaze moved to the other students in the room. "It will be called "The Spirit of West Tech!" The three thespians began to clap their hands. "And it will be used to bomb those heathens back to Hades where they belong."

I joined in the applause and since we could be heard clapping over the microphone the whole school began to clap. You could hear the thunder of the noise as it rumbled through the hallways. 4500 students were cheering and stamping their feet and clapping their hands. The whole building shook.

"My fellow students," Tuck began to speak again and the noise quieted down. "I have two more pieces of news to share with you. Sadly, one of our alumni, Greg Hudak, class of 1939, died yesterday during the Japanese sneak attack on Pearl Harbor. I remember Greg. He was a printing major who hoped to open his own shop after serving in the Navy. All of us at Tech are proud of his sacrifice."

If someone had sneezed just then the whole building would have heard it.

Tuck continued in his solemn voice. "And I am just as proud of a member of our faculty. Mr. Jameson has just received a note from Mr. Bader, our industrial arts teacher. It seems that Mr. Bader is going to be leaving West Tech in the near future." He paused for dramatic effect and looked over at me again, perhaps reading the look of surprise upon my face. "On his way to school this morning Mr. Bader stopped at the local recruiting office and joined the United States Army."

Once again there was a thunderous applause and once again I clapped my hands so hard they hurt.

"We give all our best wishes to Mr. Bader and his family," he proclaimed above the chaos. "That is the end of today's announcements."

Pat O'Leary hit "The Bells" again. "BONG, BONG, BONG."

CC Tuck put down the microphone and walked over to me. I froze in my tracks. He handed me a note. "Please give this to Mr. Bader." Then he turned his back on us and ducked back into his office.

"Good-bye Maria." I waved to her. "Thanks."

There was no time for small talk. I would have ran back to my homeroom but there was no running allowed in the halls at West Tech. But there was an unusually large amount of noise in the hallways. Each classroom was abuzz with the news of Greg Hudak and Mr. Bader.

As I walked into my home room all the guys were out of their seats, shaking Mr. Bader's hand and patting him on his back. At Tech the homerooms were segregated by gender.

"This is from Mr. Tuck," I announced as I handed

him the note. The room broke into another applause.

"That's the last time I send you on an important assignment," Mr. Bader scolded me. "You weren't supposed to read my note to the entire student body," He read Tuck's note, folded it and put it in his shop apron.

"Tell it to Mr. Jameson, he's the blabbermouth," I responded. Then I shook his hand. "What does Tuck have to say?"

The whole room instantly became quiet. "He just says "good luck," Mr. Bader looked away. I could tell he was holding something back.

"That's all?"

Mr. Bader sat down at his desk, took the note out of his apron and unfolded it. He had a serious look on his face. So we all sat down and waited for him to compose himself. We considered ourselves lucky to have him as a homeroom teacher. He was not much older than we were and we thought of him as one of our friends, a stand-up guy you could go to with your problems. We waited for him to come clean.

"If you guys really want to know," he stretched it out. "Tuck says he is proud of me and promises to keep me on the school payroll the rest of the year and send my paycheck to my family even if I am in the Army. I'm not sure how he can do that but if there is a way I guess Mr. Tuck will figure it out."

And then the bell rang. So we left Mr. Bader and the

war behind for more mundane tasks.

Later in the day President Roosevelt's famous "Day of Infamy" speech, declaring war on Japan, was also broadcast over the school's loudspeakers. But for us, the President's speech was a poor second cousin to C.C. Tucks's announcement.

We all realized that our high school would never be the same again.

CHAPTER NINE:
The Key

Once the shock of Pearl Harbor wore off, life at Tech returned to a somewhat normal routine. But I could not get Mr. Fleming off my mind. I did not trust him. He was up to something.

But was it sinister or just illegal? Maybe he was only trying to make a little extra money on the side. Teachers were never paid enough, even back then.

The more I thought about Fleming, the more I became obsessed with him. After all, there was a war going on. I felt bad that we never followed up on the strangers taking pictures at the Bomber Plant. Or the guys jumping off the boat at Edgewater Park. Mr. Fleming was right under our noses. It was time to be patriotic and investigate the situation.

But how? I decided to return to his chemistry class on my own. No use dragging Mr. Friedrich into this. I would just pretend to be doing a follow-up story for *The Tatler*.

Suddenly, I began to feel like Clark Kent. What would Superman do in this situation? I decided to surprise him, maybe catch him off guard. Instead of showing up after school I'd stop by his class before school started.

The Thursday after Pearl Harbor I popped my head into his classroom at 8:15, fifteen minutes before the first bell. I was not even sure what to ask him. I was going to wing it.

"Mr. Fleming, do you have a minute?" I said from the doorway.

He was sitting at his desk, studying some papers. When he saw me he stood up a bit too quickly and shuffled the papers together so I could not see them. Then he met me at the door.

"Mr. Blazek, what brings you here?" He shook my hand clumsily as if I was an adult. I could tell he was a bit uncomfortable.

"Remember the story I wrote about you for *The Tatler*?" I invited myself inside his classroom.

"Oh yes, it was quite good. I meant to compliment you on it." Fleming stepped back and let me enter. Then he walked over to the laboratory so I would follow him. I took a quick look at his desk. I sensed he was guiding me away from it.

"Well, it was pretty short, a lot of students wanted a bit more to chew on." On top of his desk was a green lab book with a key on top of it. The same large round skeleton key I saw him use to lock up his cabinet the last time I interviewed him.

"Chew on?" He started adjusting a Bunsen burner.

"You know, we have a famous professor in our midst and they know very little about you?"

"What do they want to know?" He gave me a look I had not seen before. It was very serious, even a bit threatening.

"Oh the usual. How you became a teacher, why you like chemistry, what's your favorite color."

"My favorite color? Who cares about that?"

"That's just an example. We call it a personality profile. I have to go to class. Could we sit down sometime and do a real interview?"

He fiddled with the Bunsen burner for a few moments before looking up at me. You could tell he was mulling over his response. "We'll see. I am very busy right now, you know, with the war and all. I do not have much free time."

"Could you at least think about it? Let me know in a few days?" I asked him.

Mr. Fleming walked me back to the classroom. The skeleton key on his desk was calling my name.

If only I had x-ray vision like Superman. Then I could see what kind of stuff he kept in his cabinet. Maybe he was hiding a secret formula. Or a human brain preserved in formaldehyde like in one of those Bela Lugosi movies.

"That will be fine. I'll come by *The Tatler* office if I can squeeze it in," he told me. It was obvious Mr. Fleming did not like me dropping in on him.

A couple students started trickling in early. "I'm only there ninth period," I said as I exited the room.

"I'll remember that." He turned away from me quite abruptly and went back toward his desk.

I entered the hallway that was filling up with students on their way to their first period classes. I bumped into them as I walked along, my mind in a fog. The key kept popping up in my mind.

There was only one thing to do. I was going to have to steal it.

CHAPTER TEN:
It Takes a Thief

If I were going to steal the key and look inside Mr. Fleming's secret cabinet I was going to have to do it quickly before I lost my nerve. I vowed to come back after classes and do the dirty work.

By the end of ninth period many students were heading home. But a number of them stayed after school for study hall detentions or extra-curricular activities.

I remembered from the Pearl Harbor PA announcements that Mr. Fleming was the sponsor for the radio club. And that they were meeting tenth period in the fourth floor radio room. So after leaving *The Tatler* office I took the long way to Mr. Fleming's chemistry class, wandering the hallways aimlessly.

I slowed my pace approaching his room and timed it perfectly. He was just closing the door, exiting with a briefcase tucked under his arm. I turned and walked in the opposite direction for a bit. Then after he left I walked into his room just like I was supposed to be there.

My heart was thumping so hard I thought the buttons would pop off my white shirt. I closed the door behind me and went straight to his desk. I opened the top drawer and my heart instantly slowed down. The key was not there.

I should have known. It could not be that easy. Chances were that he took it with him. Or maybe he hid it somewhere. But where? I quickly surveyed the room. I tried to think like Mr. Fleming but it was hopeless. I barely knew the guy.

I checked all the desk drawers. Nothing. Then I looked around for a hook or something. Maybe he left it out in the open? There was no reason to expect that anyone would steal it.

I finally gave up on finding the key. But since I was already in his room I took a look at the lab book on the desk. Maybe there was a clue in his experiments?

The book contained the lesson plans for his classes. I could be in big trouble for looking at those. If I was caught it would look like I was cheating in my chemistry class. Tuck would have a field day with that one.

As I fumbled through the pages thinking about how I was destroying my whole high school career on a crazy whim the key magically fell out of the book. It had been tucked inside a cardboard compartment on the inside of the front cover.

"Eureka!"

I grabbed the key and almost ran over to the cabinet. But just as I made my move the doorknob began to twist. Busted.

I froze in shock, looking for a table to hide under. But it was too late. The door slowly opened. But instead of Mr. Fleming, it was Lazarus, the janitor, who entered the room.

Alleluia, praise the Lord and pass the mashed potatoes. I knew Lazarus. He was an Italian immigrant that I had worked with my sophomore year. We delivered packages in the mornings before school started, taking supplies to the various departments. Chemicals, paper, tools, all the materials needed to keep Tech running smoothly.

"Hello Lazarus," I smiled.

"Victor, my boy, what are you doing here?"

"Oh, I just forgot my homework," I picked up Mr. Fleming's lab book and put it on top of my history textbook. "How are you doing? How's your wife?"

"Oh, she not doing so good. Still has the shingles. Doctor can do nothing for her."

"Give her my best, I have to be going. Good seeing you Lazarus."

"Take care, Victor."

Lazarus was carrying his toolbox. He was obviously on a repair mission. I did not stay long enough to find out what he was doing there. As soon as the door closed behind me I put the key back in its lab book compartment and wondered what to do next.

I would have to wait until Lazarus was done to put

Mr. Fleming's lab book back where it belonged. I thought about waiting until morning but could not take that chance. Mr. Fleming might stop back after the radio club meeting. I was playing with fire and unsure what to do next.

What should I do with the mysterious key that I wanted so badly? Now that I had it I could not use it. I needed to open the cabinet, but when, where and how? Then it hit me. We could make another key right here at Tech and I could then open the cabinet at my leisure.

I raced down to the drafting room hoping Ed Gorski would still be there. The drafting room was in the basement just off the cafeteria.

Fortunately for me, Ed and a couple other students were hunched over their drawing boards. Now that football season was over he was playing catch-up on his class projects.

"Hey T-square," I slapped him on his back, getting straight to the point. "I need a favor."

"Right, that's the only time I hear from you is when you need something."

He was messing with me but I was not in the mood.

"Don't give me any of that crap," I told him. "This is important."

Ed could tell by the expression on my face that I meant business. "Sure, sure, what do you need?"

"I need you to make a copy of this key," I pulled it

out of the lab book. "Can you draw me the specs?"

"Why not take it to a locksmith?"

"I don't have the time, I need it right now."

"Right now?"

"This very instant. Can you do it or not?"

"Okay, give me a second."

Ed cleared the project he was working on off his desk. He hung up his triangle, t-square, and slide rule and took a new sheet of drafting paper from a large roller. They were the kind of supplies Lazarus and I had schlepped around early in the morning my sophomore year.

He took the key and placed it on the special drafting paper that was filled with intricate little boxes. He took a number 2 lead pencil and traced its outline. Then he measured its depth and thickness and made a few notes.

"Is that all you need?"

"For now, but I'll need the specs so I can take it over to the pattern makers. Can you do it by tomorrow morning?"

"I can do it right now if you want to wait."

"No time, thanks."

"What's this all about?"

"I'll tell you later. But you can't tell anyone."

"If you say so."

"See you in the morning."

"Okey-dokey."

By the time I reached Gorski's drafting room I had already formulated my plan. Ed would draw the key's measurements, then I would take it to the pattern-making class where they would make a wood model. From there I would take the model to the foundry where they would make a mold out of sand, then pour hot metal into the mold. After the metal cooled I would make one final stop at the machine shop where they would grind out the imperfections and voila, I'd have my own copy of Mr. Fleming's cabinet key to use whenever I wished.

It might sound a bit complicated but that was a typical project for many of Tech's senior shop majors. I knew the routine because of a few of my upper class friends did it the previous year.

I would worry about the rest of the details later. I had to take the lab book back to Mr. Fleming's desk by the end of tenth period. I decided not to wait until Lazarus was finished. I needed to go back in and fake him out, kind of like using one of my wrestling moves to confuse the opposition.

I knocked on Fleming's door.

"Who there?" Lazarus asked from inside.

"It's me, Victor." I entered again.

"What bring you back, Mr. Blazek?"

Lazarus was on a ladder working on a burned-out

overhead light. He was doing more than changing the bulb. There were loose wires hanging down.

"I took the wrong lab book last time," I said.

"You seem very confused for such a young man," Lazarus said, looking down at me for an instant, then going back to work.

I quickly put the lab book on top of Fleming's desk, then took an empty one from a pile of spares in the back of the room.

"I heard oranges are good for shingles," I told Lazarus on the way out.

"We tried that." He shook his head, looking back down at me. "You graduate this year?"

"Yeah, in June, I hope."

"You'll do well, you a hard worker."

"Thanks, Lazarus. See you around the ship."

"What that you say?"

"Never mind."

I closed the door with a sigh of relief. But I still had not seen the inside of Fleming's cabinet. The curiosity was gripping me like the proverbial cat on a hot tin roof. I was determined to see what Mr. Fleming was up to, come hell or high water.

CHAPTER ELEVEN:
The Foundry

You're not going to find many high schools today that have its own foundry. Or auto shop, greenhouse and printing press for that matter. But West Tech had all that and then some.

Everyone declared a major junior year, much like at a university. Then you spent four periods a day senior year working on your specialty. Normally, that meant either your morning or your afternoon was spent in one room, learning a skill.

My pal Ed Gorski, the draftsman, had the specs for Mr. Fleming's key ready for me first thing in the morning. That was easy, he was my friend. Convincing the foundry guys to make me a key would be a bit more difficult.

The foundry was located in another part of the basement. I arrived there early, fifteen minutes before the first bell. Mr. Urlander was standing by his door already wearing his gray shop coat, waiting for his troops to arrive. The foundry was the dirtiest room in the school, kind of like a mini-steel mill. Yet Mr. Urlander wore a white shirt and tie under his coat just like all the rest of the male faculty. He was a burly, foul-mouthed, grizzly bear of a guy, and his students loved him.

I wanted to intercept Joe Kilbane before he went into class. We wrestled together sophomore year but he dropped out of the sport to work part-time in the evenings. I figured he was my best hope, my only foundry shop connection.

Joe showed up walking down the hallway with a couple of his buddies. "Hello Joe, what'd you know?" I said out of Mr. Urlander's earshot.

"Hey Slats, what brings you to the pits of West Tech?"

"I need to ask you a favor," I said to him. His two friends went into the classroom without him.

"Why don't you come in? Mr. Urlander, can my friend Victor stop in for a minute?" Joe asked him.

"As long as he's out by the time the bell rings," Mr. Urlander replied.

"No problem. Thank you sir."

I joined Joe in the foundry while he substituted his own white shirt and tie for a gray work shirt. There was a pile of sand sitting in the middle of the room, surrounded by work tables with wood molds sitting on them. The pattern makers built the molds for the sand to hold the hot metal.

The room was hot and dirty even when they weren't pouring hot metal. I talked to Joe while he fished a shop apron out of his locker.

"Joe, do you think you can make me a key, maybe do it as a class project or something?"

"What kind of key?"

"It's hard to explain but I've got the specs. T-square drew them up. One of your boys could make the mold, it's pretty simple."

"I don't know, we've got a full load of work. What's in it for me?"

"How about a couple tickets to the school play?"

"Naw, that's sissy stuff."

"What about the winter dance?" My mind was racing. I was grasping for straws and I was running out of time. I needed to be on time for my first class or risk the wrath of Tuck.

"You're getting warmer."

"What do you want Joe? Spit it out."

"A couple tickets to the dance plus a date."

"A date?"

"Yeah, with a cheerleader. You seem to know all those girls."

"Man, you're asking a lot."

"Take it or leave it. I don't need the key, you do. It sounds pretty fishy to me."

"Okay, okay, I'll try, but I can't guarantee a cheerleader. How about a band member?" I thought Doris could help me out on that score.

"I'll make the key but no delivery until you find

me a cheerleader."

"All right, all right, you're a hard guy to deal with. Here's the specs. And I need it this week."

"See, something is going on. What are you up to?"

"Nothing for you to worry about." I gave him Stash's drafting paper and took off past Mr. Urlander.

"Where's your first class?" he asked me as I was leaving.

"Room 222," I answered.

"You better hurry, son."

I took off at a fast trot. There was no running allowed at Tech. The hallways were beginning to thin out. I broke out in a cold sweat. I had enough problems, I didn't need an invitation to Tuck's track team. And where was I going to find a cheerleader who would go out with Joe Kilbane? He wasn't the sharpest pencil in the pack. Or the best looking.

I made it to first period just after the bell rang. My English teacher, Mr. Mazzini, could have given me a detention but he let me slide. Once again I'd dodged the bullet but I could feel the long shadow of Tuck looking over my shoulder. One of these days my luck was going to run out.

CHAPTER TWELVE: The Machine Shop

The West Tech machine shop was also in the basement. It was a large collection of lathes and grinding machines, all operating at the same time, churning up a cacophony of metallic noise.

But it did have one advantage over the other basement classes. In fact, it was an advantage over all the other majors. It was located just opposite the girl's gym.

The machine shop guys loved to stand by the door and strut their stuff like peacocks, vying for the girl's attention. This was especially prevalent between classes when the girls were filing into their locker room and just afterwards when they filed out of the locker room into the gym, dressed in their blue shorts and T-shirts. They had to use a short section of the hallway and it was the most popular piece of real estate in the whole school.

Poor Mr. Pizadazz, the lord of the machine shop, had a full time job all day long shooing his troops into the classroom. It was probably the source of his cranky disposition. He could be mean at times but for the most part he understood the attraction between the youthful sexes.

Joe Kilbane had delivered my key on the promise of a date with a cheerleader. I still had to work out the details but he let me have the key when I explained the urgency of the situation. I told him it was for the war effort and he caved.

The machine shop was the final step in the process. They would grind off any raw edges and check it for any deficiencies. That was standard operating procedure.

Once again I needed a connection and fortunately I had one. Just like the Irish guys ran the foundry, the Italian guys controlled the machine shop. But they had a more formal pecking order and fortunately the godfather owed me a favor.

Tony "The Knife" Bambino sat next to me in tenth grade algebra class. If I had not been a bit open, shall we say, with my test answers he would still be sitting in Miss Krugar's room, attempting to decipher logarithms.

"Hey Paisan," I shouted over the hallway noise between classes. "How's it hanging?"

He was standing in the doorway already wearing his shop apron. His dress shirt was gone and his white T-shirt sleeves were rolled up to show off his huge biceps. His left arm revealed a long scar from a knife fight that was a souvenir of his rough and tumble youth. It was also the source of his nickname.

He liked to rub it when he talked to you, just to let you know how tough he was. Two of his lieutenants,

Joe and Louie, shared his doorway location, standing a few feet behind him. During the day they would follow him around the school like a couple of puppy dogs.

"Hey Slats, move out of the way. You're blocking the view." Tony waved his big hand sideways.

The girls were filing into the gym, some giggling, some smiling, some flirting with the Great Bambino as he made risque comments to them.

"Sorry Tony, but I need a favor."

"Not a good time to talk, Victor. Tell it to Louie." He jerked his thumb in the direction of his first lieutenant, Louie Marconi, who I also knew from a math class. He played the trumpet in a local swing band.

I moved out of the doorway in deference to Tony's wishes and pulled Louie away from the feminine scenery.

"Louie, old buddy, I need a favor from Tony."

"What's with you, Slats? Can't you see we're busy?"

"Just give him this key and these drawings and have him fine tune the key. Just like it was a class project."

"Hey, screwball, you don't give Tony no orders, capiche?" He was acting the tough guy but I wasn't buying it. I knew that without his connection to Tony he was just another sissy musician.

"Listen Louie, Tony owes me big time from algebra class and he knows it. I don't have time to talk but this is important." I handed him the key and Ed's drawings.

"Okay, Slats, but now you owe me big time."

"Maybe I can help your band get a gig for the next school dance."

"That might work." Louie smiled, his demeanor changed considerably.

"I have to run to class. Don't let me down."

This time I was cutting it closer than when I visited the foundry. It was fifth period after lunch and I had to go all the way to the third floor for my chemistry class. I darted up the back stairway, worrying about Mr. Tuck all the way.

Fortunately, he usually stood by the front hallway near his office between classes. Unfortunately, this was one of those days when school business took him to the back of the school.

I had raced up the steps two at a time and thought I was home free when I hit the third floor. Then the bell rang. The halls were already empty. I was praying that Mr. Seibring, my chemistry teacher, would cut me some slack.

He never had the chance. Mr. Tuck was coming out of Mr. Fleming's class of all places. Right next to my class. I walked right into him.

"Where are you going, young man?" he asked me, all six foot four of him, towering over me.

"My chemistry class, right there," I stammered.

"Don't I know you?"

"Victor Blazek, sir. I write for *The Tatler*."

"Oh yes, I've heard some good things about you. But you know we can't tolerate tardiness."

"Yes sir." I thought he was going to give me a break. I was afraid to say anything that might ruin my chances.

"You're a senior?"

"Yes sir."

"And you've never been on my track team?"

"No sir."

"Then I'd say you're a bit overdue. If I let you walk the halls between bells the next thing you know everyone will be doing it."

"Yes, sir."

"Be in my office at 7 a.m. sharp tomorrow morning. One or two days should be enough unless you're late again. Understand."

"Yes sir."

Then he turned his back and walked away. My luck had run out.

CHAPTER THIRTEEN:
Tuck's Track Team

Bright and early the next morning I reported to Principal Tuck's office with the rest of the school's common criminals. We were minor offenders, misdemeanors at best, in the hierarchy of Tech discipline.

The Track Team was Tuck's way of dealing with such infractions as tardiness, gum chewing, cigarette smoking or dress code violations. He did not have to deal with a lot of rule breakers because most of the discipline was handled by the teachers in the classrooms.

The teachers usually offered you a couple options. You could take some swats or a few detentions. Back in those days there were a lot more male teachers than today. And Principal Tuck liked to hire big guys, gym teacher types, who did not take any crap from their students.

Each male teacher had his own signature paddle that was made in the woodshop class. The paddle usually hung from a leather strap in a prominent area at the front of the room. Just the sight of it would make you think twice about acting up in class.

Today even paddling preschoolers is frowned upon by our social leaders. But back then paddling in the school was just an extension of the discipline style used in most homes. And it worked.

The swats at Tech were brutal. Even the toughest guys tried to avoid them. Early in the semester the teacher would finger the class troublemaker, call him to the front of the class and make him bend over, grabbing the edge of the teacher's desk. A couple well-placed smacks to his buttocks would often bring tears to the eyes of the offender. It sent a powerful message to the rest of the class and made the teacher's job much easier for the rest of the school year.

The female teachers, who were a distinct minority at Tech, would just pass the paddling task on to the assistant principal. Every day after school there would be a line of juvenile offenders outside the assistant principal's office, waiting to take their punishment. It taught us responsibility as it left our behinds with a very uncomfortable feeling.

I remember coming home one time sophomore year with a butt so red it had blisters on it. Today parents would call a lawyer. But back then I made the mistake of letting my father notice that I had a bit of trouble sitting down at the dinner table. It did not take him long to figure out why. What did he do? He added a few more smacks to my behind with his belt. I learned quickly to keep my mouth shut in the classroom and not to expect any sympathy from my parents if I caused any trouble at Tech.

At least that is the way it worked for the male students. The teachers ruled, the families backed up the teachers and the system created a safe environment for learning.

The female students were dealt with by the dean of girls. Their punishments were somewhat of a mystery to us guys but we liked to think that they never did anything wrong anyway.

As for myself, if given a choice, I always took the swats. The pain was short and sweet. Detentions were like doing time in prison. The misery was long and drawn out.

I had heard stories about Tuck's Track Team since the first day I entered Tech's hallowed halls. Yet I had somehow managed to avoid it. The school secretary, Miss Smith, checked us in. She had a list of all the runners ready to go. Once all the names were accounted for, Principal Tuck took us out to the front of the school.

"Okay gentlemen, one lap around the premises, east on Willard, north on 89th, left on Sauer Avenue behind the football field and back down West 93rd. When you come back here check in with Miss Smith and she'll make sure you make it back to class."

We all looked at him, waiting for some sort of signal to begin. We were wearing our school clothes: the white shirts, slacks, belts and dress shoes that were required as part of Tech's dress code. We were also wearing the long coats that were the style of the times. They were difficult to run in.

It was all guys, no girls. I guess today some wise guy would holler sexual discrimination but being on Tuck's track team was almost a badge of honor. In a way I was glad to finally join the ranks.

"And one more thing," C.C. Tuck added. "See the printing room on the fourth floor?" He pointed up towards the sky. "From there I can watch you the entire way. If you stop or take any shortcuts you'll be back for a whole week."

We were a diverse group of about a dozen students of various shapes and sizes. We looked at him for the signal to begin. Suddenly he pulled a starter pistol out of his pocket like a marshal in the old west. It was the kind used to start races for the track team.

"Well, what are you waiting for?" he growled as he fired the gun toward the sky. "You better not be late for first period."

So we took off down Willard Avenue in a slow trot. A few student athletes took off ahead, a few out-of-shape heavyweights dragged behind, but most of us bunched up in the middle. The course we ran would be called a city block by most people. But it was a large city block because it included the large school and its football field and stands.

There were only a few automobiles traveling the side streets carrying commuters to work. Most of Cleveland's neighborhood citizens were walking to the trolley stops. They were well aware of Tuck's Track Team and greeted us with smiles of pity for our situation. Some even waved to us like we were celebrities.

I tried striking up a conversation with a guy I knew from my history class but he would have none of it. He was too busy sucking air. I soon understood his reasoning. Talking just made the run that much more difficult.

As I broke into a regular trot like a horse delivering the Pony Express mail, I looked up at the printing room on the fourth floor. I had only been on the fourth floor a couple times in my high school career. Mostly delivering packages with Lazarus, the janitor. I wondered if Tuck was really up there looking down on us like one of the Greek gods. Zeus throwing down lightning bolts if one of us tried taking a shortcut through the teachers' parking lot. Or was it just for show since he knew none of us would have the guts to test his wrath.

At the end of the run I reported to Miss Smith, breathing hard, my heart pounding through my shirt. "Victor Blazek, present and accounted for." I tried to smile.

She checked my name off her list, not at all interested in my bland attempt at humor. "You may go to class now, Mr. Blazek."

"Is that it or do I come back tomorrow?" I had to ask. I was not sure how many days Tuck had tacked onto my sentence.

"One more day and then you're done," she said matter-of-factly, turning away from me to more pressing matters.

Damn, I thought. But then an idea struck me. The idea of all ideas. What if I split from my group, snuck inside the school and then used my key to investigate Mr. Fleming's cabinet? Turn defeat into victory, that sort of thing.

I vowed to try it the next day.

CHAPTER FOURTEEN:
The File Cabinet

Tuck's Track Team, day two. Reported to Miss Smith at 7 a.m. sharp. Took Tuck's instructions and started east on Willard Avenue. There were a couple repeat offenders like myself but also quite a few new faces.

I had picked up my key from Tony Bambino the previous evening. To my surprise he did not ask me for any favors. I guess he remembered how I carried him in algebra class.

All he said was, "now we're even."

I said, "thanks," and that was that. No more favors from Big Tony.

As the pack turned the corner on West 89th street I made my move. I fell considerably behind the group but none of the other students seemed to notice. They were too intent on paying their dues.

I figured the corner would be the hardest part of the race to watch from the fourth floor, if Tuck was actually up there. And I had an excuse ready although it would probably cost me a few extra days on the track team. I would tell him my stomach was upset and I had to go to the bathroom badly. Very badly.

Instead of running up West 89th street I ran into the glass greenhouse used by Tech's horticulture classes. Mr. Osborne, the horticulture teacher, was busy watering the chrysanthemums for a upcoming flower show. He nurtured the indoor flowers and vegetables like they were his own offspring.

I ran right past him without stopping for an explanation. He turned, looked at me and just shook his head. I went through the greenhouse and used its entrance into the school. It was probably the only way to sneak inside Tech before school started. Anyone else who came in early had to register at the front office and sit in the cafeteria until the first bell.

I ran up the stairs to the third floor chemistry class. Running all those stairs reminded me of our wrestling class drills. I tried not to think about the danger involved and the risk to my education. I knew in my gut that I was doing the right thing.

The third floor was eerily empty. It took me back to tenth grade when I delivered packages, walking down the empty halls in this huge old building with only a noisy pull cart as my companion. I learned a lot that year, about myself as well as the school.

I slipped into Mr. Fleming's room, half expecting

him to be waiting for me. Luckily, he was nowhere in sight. I had to act fast. I pulled the key from my pocket, dropped it on the floor and the sound reverberated through the empty classroom like a fire cracker. My hand shook as I picked up the key and tried to put it into the cabinet lock.

It was not a perfect fit but after a little jiggling the door swung open. Eureka. I felt a sigh of relief after so much effort but the sense of success was soon replaced by fear and trepidation. The cabinet was stocked with tall rolls of paper, held together with rubber bands.

I looked to the door, all was quiet, so I took a couple rolls over to the desk and opened them up. They were blueprints to buildings. Something did not add up. I expected secret formulas to powerful new weapons. Why would a chemistry teacher care about Cleveland's buildings?

I found the legend for the blueprints in the lower corner of the first pages. The first roll was for the Alcoa Aluminum plant on Harvard Avenue. The second one was for the Republic Steel mills in the Flats.

I looked to the door once again. I could feel the seconds ticking away. I rolled them up and put them back in the cabinet. Should I grab a couple more? What the hell, I knew it was dangerous but my curiosity was out of control.

Two more rolls revealed two more buildings, my

brother-in-law's Sohio oil refinery in the Flats and the bomber plant by the airport. As I rolled them back up it struck me like a bolt of lighting.

The bomber plant! The foreigners taking pictures of the B-17's at the Air Show over the summer. Was Mr. Fleming a spy?

The Alcoa plant made the aluminum needed to construct the airplanes at the bomber plant. Republic Steel forged the metal to build tanks, cannons and ships. Sohio took the crude oil from Pennsylvania and turned it into the gasoline and diesel fuel used to run the war machine.

My heart started racing. There had to be an explanation but what was it and whose side was Mr. Fleming on? I put the rolls back, locked the cabinet and listened for noise in the hallway before opening the door.

The students had already been let out of the cafeteria and were beginning to roam the halls. I scooted down the stairs and went out the back door. Then I sprinted around the corner of West 93rd to build up a load of steam so that by the time I came in the front door to report to Miss Smith I was winded.

"Where have you been?" Miss Smith asked me. "You're the last of the track team."

"My stomach was upset so I had to take a break. My mom made me eggs this morning to give me energy but I think it backfired."

"Well, you better hurry or you'll be late for class and back here again tomorrow."

"Thanks," I said. No sign of Tuck. Mission accomplished.

But what was I to do with my ill-gotten information? Call the police and tell them I broke into Mr. Fleming's cabinet? This would take some heavy thinking. I needed to confide in someone. Mr. Friedrich maybe? I needed more proof before I could tell him what I did.

Doris. She would understand. She had a sharp mind, a woman's intuition and she knew Mr. Fleming from chemistry class. Maybe she could help me out.

CHAPTER FIFTEEN:
The Roller Rink

It was Friday night and the best place to find the students from West Tech on a cold winter weekend was the Denison Avenue Roller Rink.

You could take a date, go with some friends, or just show up on your own. The Roller Rink was a great place for guys and gals to meet up. Many couples who later married and raised families could trace the roots of their relationships to the Denison Avenue Roller Rink.

I went there looking for Doris. I had been thinking about Mr. Fleming's blueprints all day and it was making me crazy. I needed to talk to someone about them. If I couldn't find Doris I was going to tell Ed or Frank.

I lived on West 47th off Denison and the rink was on West 65th so it wasn't a long walk. In fact, I kind of enjoyed it. The brisk cold air cleared my head and I reviewed all that had happened to me since the school year started.

I had to decide what to do with my information about Mr. Fleming. Go to the cops? Then I'd have to explain breaking into his file cabinet. Since I was a student and he was a famous chemist, that might backfire on me.

Confide in Mr. Friedrich? How well did I know Mr. Friedrich? Maybe he was friends with Mr. Fleming, maybe even his partner in crime. Weren't they both a couple of krauts? Could I trust him not to rat on me?

I needed more evidence but I did not know how to find it.

I walked into the Roller Rink. The place was hopping. The large "Mighty Wurlitzer" organ was belting out a boogie-woogie beat. The kids moved around and around, many dancing to the sound on their skates.

Me, I was just an average skater. I could go around the rink all right and hold a girl with two hands but none of that fancy stuff. I kept out of the way of the swingers and boppers.

I laced my skates and kept my eyes peeled for Doris. She hung with a group of her friends called The Bachelorettes. She told me there were six of them and they took the name because of the guy shortage caused by the war.

Every day since Pearl Harbor the newspapers showed lines of young men going down to the Terminal Tower, the local train station, on their way to basic training. Outside of high school there were fewer and fewer guys on the streets of the city.

My first couple times around the rink I was too busy trying to keep from falling to look for Doris. Besides, the place was crowded and I was in constant danger of being knocked down by a fancy dancer.

Once I did begin looking in earnest I found her pretty quick. She was flea hopping with a line of girls that I assumed were The Bachelorettes. I slowly worked my way toward her. A couple of her friends looked familiar, probably students at Tech, but I could not place them.

"Hello Doris," I hollered over the noise and the music after moving within range of her hearing.

"Victor." She turned excitedly to answer me.

The slight movement was just enough to upset the dynamics of her skating line. One of the girls from the back of the line lost her balance and crashed into Doris. They both went down like a ton of bricks.

Doris fell on her elbow and screamed in pain. I felt terrible since I had caused the accident with my meddling.

"Doris, are you all right?" I knelt beside her as skaters swerved to miss us. It was like an accident in the middle of a busy highway. The chances of it turning into a mass collision were great.

"I think I hit my funny bone," she was rubbing her elbow. "How's Cathy?"

Cathy was her friend. She was trying to stand up and rub her rear end at the same time. "I'm okay, I landed on my dupa," she said. "I've got a lot of padding down there."

Doris laughed with tears of pain in her eyes. We each took one of her arms and gingerly picked her up off the hard wooden floor. I blocked the traffic while Cathy guided her to the opening in the guardrail around the rink. We sat her down on one of the wooden benches that were used to tie your skates.

"You need to put some ice on it," Cathy said.

"There's plenty outside, I'll go out and find some," I said and began to take off my skates.

"Mind if I go outside with you," Doris said. " I think I'm done for the night."

"I'll unlace your skates," Cathy offered.

"Sorry Doris." I tried to smile, as I unlaced my own skates.

"It was my fault." Cathy looked up at me with big brown mournful eyes.

"It was just an accident," Doris said matter-of-factly, giving Cathy a sharp glance.

I suddenly remembered where I'd seen Cathy. She liked to hang around outside the boy's gym at Tech. She had a reputation for being boy crazy.

Once we had our shoes on, Doris thanked Cathy and told her in so many words to go join the rest of the Bachelorettes on the skate floor. It was a side of Doris I had not seen before. Cathy gave Doris a snotty look as she left us.

Doris and I went outside. We walked around to the

back of the rink where a few cars were parked. I found a couple of icicles hanging from the edge of the roof and broke one off. Doris rolled up her sleeve revealing a large red bump on her elbow.

I pulled a handkerchief from my pocket and wrapped it around the icicle.

"Don't worry, it's clean."

"I hope so." She laughed.

"My mother makes me carry it but I never use it," I explained. "I think it's a tradition from the old country."

"I know what you mean, OUCH!" she screamed as I applied the cold ice to her wound.

"Sorry," I said. "It might hurt for a few seconds but then it'll be okay."

"If you say so, Dr. Blazek."

"I guess I ruined your evening."

"Not really," she said softly. "But if you wanted to get me alone in the parking lot all you had to do was ask."

"Really?" I smiled at her. She smiled back. I wanted to kiss her but I was holding her arm with both hands. It was too awkward. For a few moments I did not know what to say.

"You know, I came up here looking for you," I confessed.

"Really?"

"Really."

Another awkward pause. "I wanted to ask your advice?"

"Advice?" Her smile changed to a look of disappointment.

"You're one of the few people I feel I can confide in."

"Really?" Her smile returned.

"Really."

"What did you want to ask me about?"

"How does your arm feel?"

"It's beginning to feel better." She looked up at me and brought her body closer to mine. I could smell her perfume. "But my arm's going numb."

"That's probably enough ice." I untied my handkerchief and threw the icicle in a snow bank. Doris rolled her sleeve back down.

"Well?"

"This is hard to explain," I started nervously. "First, you have to promise me you won't tell anyone else unless you ask me first."

"Sure," she answered excitedly.

"I mean it, Doris. This isn't high school gossip. This is important stuff."

"Okay," she said solemnly.

"Here it is then. I think Mr. Fleming may be a spy."

"A spy?" A puzzled look swept across her face. She pulled away from me as if she was angry but then she regained her composure. "What do you mean?"

"I think he's working for the Nazis and I don't know what to do about it."

"I like Mr. Fleming. I had him for chemistry last year. Why do you think he's a spy?"

I explained to her how I broke into his cabinet and found the plans for all the defense plants in Cleveland. I gave her the short version, not telling her that I made my own key.

"If he finds out you were in his cabinet you could be expelled," Doris cautioned.

"I know. That's why you can't tell anyone. I don't know what to do next."

"Maybe I could help you," she moved her body close to mine again. "It's getting cold out here."

I put my arms around her coat. She raised her face up to mine.

"What could you do?"

"I could watch Mr. Fleming for you."

"You'd do that for me?"

"I'd do anything for you.'

"Really?"

"Really."

Our faces were so close that we could feel each other's misty breaths. I was about to try to kiss her when she spoke again.

"Besides, my sister works at the bomber plant. Maybe she would know what to do."

"She does?"

"Yes, my uncle got her the job. She replaced a guy

in accounting who was drafted."

"Is your sister anything like you?"

"Some people say we're identical twins."

"Then I'd love to talk to her."

Our faces kept moving closer and closer together. By this time Mr. Fleming was the furthest thing from my mind. Doris closed her eyes. I moved my lips to hers.

We kissed slowly. The first time for just a few seconds. I opened my eyes to look at her and her eyes were still closed. So I kissed her again. This time it seemed to last forever.

When we finally pulled apart I didn't know what to say. "Maybe we should go inside."

"If you really want to."

"Not really, do you?"

"Not really."

So we kissed some more. I'd never kissed anyone like that before. By the time we rejoined the Bachelorettes inside I had a partner in my pursuit of truth, justice and the American Way.

I felt like Superman.

CHAPTER SIXTEEN:
Doris' Home

Doris did not waste any time. She invited me to her home on the following evening, Saturday night, to meet her sister. She lived in the opposite direction from Tech than I did.

I lived east of the school, closer to downtown or the inner city as some liked to call it. She lived west of the school, closer to Cleveland's outskirts, almost in the suburbs. When I walked out of my front door I could smell the smokestacks from the steel mills in the Flats and the cow manure from the neighborhood stock-yards. When she walked out her door she could smell the roses next to her front porch.

I probably forgot to mention that West Tech was what we call a "magnet" school today. By that I mean it was not a neighborhood school. If you lived on the west side of Cleveland you could go to your neigh-borhood high school or you could go to West Tech. (East Tech provided a similar option to kids on the east side of town.)

Not having its own district just added another

weapon in Tech's disciplinary arsenal. Just like at a parochial school, principal C. C. Tuck could throw a troublemaker out of Tech and make him go back to his neighborhood high school, like Abraham Lincoln or John Marshall.

Tech's reputation was so great that many students who lived near the city's border commuted quite a long way to attend it. There were even instances where a student's parents moved to the suburbs before the student graduated but they kept sending their kids to Tech anyway.

The differences between Doris' neighborhood and mine were noticeable. Houses in my neighborhood were smaller and closer together than in hers. Mine was a two-family double. Hers was a three-bedroom single. Our backyard was the size of a postage stamp. Hers was big enough to play a game of touch football.

Doris only had to share her living quarters with one sister. You've already heard about my siblings. Let's just say Doris' household was much more subdued than mine. Maybe refined is the better word. Okay, to be honest, I lived in a madhouse while she lived in an almost normal environment.

Her father played the piano at some local night-clubs. Doris and her mother sang in the church choir. My parents could barely speak English. Theirs was a house of musical voices. Mine was a house of screaming siblings. And we had another family full of screamers living right above us.

Doris' sister, Evelyn, had graduated from Tech a few years before us. She majored in bookkeeping and once the defense industry heated up she was hired to replace a guy who was drafted while working at the bomber plant.

Like I said, there was a shortage of young males because of the war and young women were filling their ranks in the workforce. And they were making meal ticket-type wages. Suddenly a young girl could make almost as much money as her father. It was quite a shock to the older generation, who were often immigrants from the old country where such a situation was impossible.

Doris and I sat down at the kitchen table as Evelyn boiled some water on the gas stove for tea. Their parents were in the living room listening to *The Burns and Allen* radio show.

"Doris said you wanted to ask me about the bomber plant," Evelyn smiled. "If you're looking for a job I have to admit I don't have much influence."

"I guess Doris didn't tell you," I looked over at her. "I'm looking more for advice."

"What kind of advice?" she poured the hot water into our cups and then made one for herself.

I stirred my tea for a second wondering how to put

it. I should have rehearsed this earlier but I was so intent on seeing Doris that I came to her home ill-prepared.

"Well, what would you do if you thought someone was spying on the bomber plant?'

"That's easy. Go to the FBI." Evelyn sat down at the table with us.

"What, just call J. Edgar Hoover? What if you don't have any real proof and what you do have you obtained by somewhat questionable means?"

"Such as?" She put her elbows on the table, held her chin up with her knuckles and stared at me intently.

"Such as breaking into a teacher's cabinet." I looked into the other room to make sure their parents were not listening. I thought it would be their duty to turn me in if they knew what I had done. It sounded worse talking about it than it did at the time I was doing it.

"A teacher?" Evelyn blew on her tea to cool it off and looked over at Doris who took a sip. I just kept stirring mine, staring at the tea bag that was coming apart.

"Victor found a bunch of blueprints for Cleveland's defense plants," Doris explained.

"That doesn't mean anything," Evelyn countered. "He could have all kinds of reasons."

"But he's up to something," I told her. "I just can't put my finger on it."

"He needs more proof," Doris added. "Any ideas?"

"Did he have a blueprint for the bomber plant?"

"Yep."

"I wonder how he got that? And if he's allowed to have it? Maybe I'll ask around at work, find the right person to run it by?"

"That sounds like a good idea," I said. "But please don't use my name."

"Something doesn't sound right, does it Evelyn?" Doris asked.

"Now that you mention it, something does sound fishy. Those plans should be top secret with the war on and everything."

"See what I mean?"

"I'll see what I can do."

By this time our tea had cooled off so we could sip it down. After a few more sips Evelyn had another question.

"What's this Mr. Fleming like?"

"He's a strange bird. But he's supposed to be working on a project for the government."

"Well, maybe that explains the blueprints."

"But his project has something to do with explosives," I said.

"What would that have to do with defense plants?" Doris asked.

"It is curious," Evelyn stood up. "But I have to go, I have a date tonight." She looked out the kitchen window as a car's headlights lit up the backyard.

"Thanks," I said.

The car began to beep its horn.

"Is it Tom?" Doris asked with a smirk.

"Yes, it's Tom, but it's none of your business, Miss Noseypants," Evelyn said as she put on her coat.

"Oops, maybe we should spy on her?" Doris laughed.

"Tom's leaving for the Navy in two weeks so you just leave us alone. Tell mom and dad I went out."

"Boy, someone's touchy." Doris smirked.

"Nice meeting you Evelyn," I said. "Goodnight."

"Goodnight Victor, you be nice to Doris." With that she went out the door.

"Thanks for introducing us, Doris. I think asking her was a good idea."

"I like to give her a hard time but she has a pretty good head on her shoulders. Would you like to play cards?"

Doris pulled a deck of cards out of a drawer and we played rummy for a couple of hours, laughing about Tech and our fellow students. We forgot about the war and Mr. Fleming and the FBI.

Time passed quickly in her presence. Her parents drifted in and out of the kitchen and we became acquainted. By the time I left for home I felt like I was a member of her family.

"Bye Victor," Doris opened the back door for me while her parents remained in the living room.

I could feel the snow crunch under my shoes as I buttoned up my winter coat. I turned to say goodbye.

Suddenly Doris flung her arms around me and gave me a kiss like there was no tomorrow and said, "I love you, Victor."

"I love you too, Doris," I heard myself saying. Where that came from I did not know. But it gave me a whole lot to think about on the trolley ride home.

CHAPTER SEVENTEEN:
Christmas Break

The following week was the last week of school before Christmas break. There was a lot I wanted to accomplish. Besides studying for classes and writing for *The Tatler* I was working on an article for *The Argosy*, Tech's literary magazine.

It was something I had wanted to do since I first read the magazine my first year at Tech. *The Argosy* came out only once a semester so it was too late for the fall issue and the spring issue had an early deadline. So Christmas break was my last chance for immortality before I graduated in June.

My story was about my brother Johnny's pigeon racing hobby. All my siblings had hobbies despite our cramped quarters. Johnny raced pigeons in the garage. Andy developed his own photos in a darkroom he constructed in the basement. Willy built a pond in the back yard before he died so we each took turns taking care of it. It made my mother happy. And each sister had a craft like sewing, knitting or baking.

Besides interviewing Johnny and learning the pigeon racing business I also needed to find an artist. I wanted a nifty illustration to go with my story. It was like writing for *The Saturday Evening Post* or *Esquire*.

And then there was Mr. Fleming. I figured Christmas break was the perfect time to try my hand at a little detective work like Sherlock Holmes. Besides, it was a good excuse to hang out with Doris.

First, I had to find out where Mr. Fleming lived. There had to be a record of it in the school office. But how to get it? It was not the kind of information the school administration gave out easily.

Luckily, Doris had a friend who worked as one of the student helpers in the main office. Doris told her I needed the information for a story I was working on for *The Tatler*. Something about how the faculty was going to spend their holidays.

Her friend, Lucille, bought it and gave her Mr. Fleming's address. Doris was becoming my sidekick on the Fleming case, kind of like Dr. Watson to Sherlock Holmes.

The first Saturday afternoon of Christmas break neither of us was busy so we decided to case out Mr. Fleming's house.

He lived on Clifton Avenue in Lakewood, the suburb just to the west of Cleveland along the shores of Lake Erie. It was a pretty ritzy area for someone living on a teacher's salary. Maybe he was supplementing his income with foreign money? I had to find out what he was up to.

Doris and I took the trolley down Clifton Avenue. Our plan was to ride by the house, locate it, then get off the trolley and walk by it on the other side of the street. It was cold and windy so the chances of him spotting us were slim. Even if he did we could just be visiting relatives in the neighborhood. And we actually had some.

Mr. Fleming's home was a modest two-story brick house with a large front porch. It was on the north side of the street, the same side as Lake Erie, but not directly on the lake. There were a couple other streets between Mr. Fleming's house and the lake.

After we jumped off the trolley we walked on the south side of Clifton Avenue, taking a closer look at his house.

"Isn't that an antenna on top of his roof?" I asked Doris.

"Looks like it."

"He must have a ham radio."

"Well, he does run the radio club," she offered.

"Very suspicious."

"What should we do next?" she asked me.

"You tell me. It's too cold to stand around here and wait for him."

"You're right we need a place to hide. Maybe a car?"

"Good idea, we could park it on a side street like a

couple detectives." I was really warming up to the idea.

"Know anyone who owns a car?" she asked me.

"My buddy Frank. He's a car nut but he loves his Dodge. I don't know if he'd let me borrow it. How about you?"

"Just my dad, but he won't let me get a driver's license because I'm a girl."

"My brother helped me get my license but that was the last time he let me use his car. Would your dad let me borrow his if we told him it was for something important?"

"Like what?"

"We'd need a good story. Maybe your sister could help us out?"

"Evelyn? Yeah, she told me she likes you. My father kind of favors her because she's the oldest."

"Great. If we put our minds together I bet we can come up with something," I told her as I put my arm around her waist. "I'm glad you want to help me with this."

"My pleasure." She smiled as she moved her body in close to mine. We walked to the nearest trolley stop and on the way home planned our next move in the case of "The Mysterious Mr. Fleming."

CHAPTER EIGHTEEN: The Stakeout

It took us a week to find a car. We thought about asking Doris' dad if we could use his but we soon gave up on that idea. I did not really know him that well and only knew Doris a short time. It was a bit too much.

So we borrowed Frank's car. Of course, it was not without a struggle. His 1936 Dodge Coupe was his baby. I don't remember ever going over to his house to visit and not finding him out in the garage, adding some new gizmo to its engine or waxing its body.

It took a small bribe for him to let us use it for a couple of hours. The bribe was a collection of gas stamps I was able to finagle from various friends and family. During the war years gas was rationed and you needed a stamp to purchase it. The stamps were hard to come by so he appreciated the gesture. I could not afford to repay him for more than the gas we used but the gas stamps gave him the opportunity to purchase a few more gallons if he wanted.

I also had to promise to have the car back by 7 p.m. He had a hot date with his girlfriend and if we screwed that up he was going to kill us with his bare hands. Those were his exact words.

It was Wednesday night, exactly one week before Christmas. Doris and I were parked on Virginia Avenue, a side street that dead-ended into Clifton Avenue from the south. From our location we could see Mr. Fleming's house on the northern side of the street.

What we were looking for I didn't have a clue. But hanging out with Doris was becoming more important to me than spying on Mr. Fleming.

I'd brought along my brother Andy's 35 mm Argus camera in case we caught Mr. Fleming doing something suspicious. If my brother knew I had it he would have really let me have it. He paid a lot of money for it before he went into the Army and even the film was expensive.

Jack Norris had been teaching me some photo skills since I took the Charity game pictures. He told me that 35 mms were the coming thing but they were hard to develop. If I did take an important picture I'd probably have to take him into my confidence but we'd cross that bridge if we came to it.

We had to leave the car running to keep warm but Frank had the Dodge's motor running like a Swiss watch. It almost purred. And it had a radio. We were listening to the Glenn Miller Band on radio station WGAR. The sun was setting into Lake Erie behind Mr. Fleming's house. We could not see the scenic lake view but we watched the lazy clouds turning red and purple.

"Nice night," I said softly, breaking the silence. We spoke just above a whisper, as if Mr. Fleming could hear us even though we were a good distance from his house.

"It is." Doris smiled. Her cloth coat was unbuttoned. I could see her green plaid sweater, a Christmas color.

"Thanks for helping me."

"My pleasure."

"Do you think I'm crazy?"

"Yes, but not about Mr. Fleming."

"Great, that makes me feel much better." I laughed.

We listened to the radio again, just enjoying each other's company. We watched the trolleys slide down Clifton Avenue, their wheels screeching against the steel rails embedded in the concrete. The slanted electric poles sticking out of the trolley's roofs sparked on the overhead wires like a free fireworks show in the early dusk. Because of gas and rubber rationing there were only a few cars on the road. It was one of the reasons we parked a so far away from Mr. Fleming's house. Automobiles stood out a bit more than normal during the war years.

After a while I gathered up enough nerve to spring my surprise on Doris. She had slid over next to me and was sitting close. The Ford's heater was working over-time and I was becoming hot.

"I think I'm going to take my coat off," I said.

"Me, too," Doris agreed.

As she moved away for a moment I slipped my hand into my coat pocket and pulled out a small box. I did-n't have a lot of experience with girlfriends and I was about as romantic as Humphrey Bogart. So instead of making a nice little speech about how much I liked her I just shoved the box in front of her face.

"Here," I said.

"What's this?" She acted surprised.

"Your Christmas present," I said.

"Isn't this a little early?" She teased me with a smile.

"I couldn't wait. I didn't know if I'd see you again before Christmas."

Doris slowly took apart the crudely wrapped pres-ent. I noticed how pretty her hands were and how neatly she manicured her fingernails.

She opened the box and pulled out a silver necklace with a Maltese cross on it. It cost me a month's worth of stocking shelves at the neighborhood market but I figured she was worth it.

"It's beautiful." She moved over next to me and gave me a kiss on the cheek. I was not used to so much affection.

"Are you sure? I'm not so good at picking out girl's stuff."

"I love it," she put it around her neck and turned her back to me. "Can you hook it for me?"

It took me a while to snap the clasp together. I had to keep pushing her long hair away from the two threads. Her hair smelled wonderful. "Thank you," she said.

She leaned her back against my shoulder and twirled the cross in her fingers. "It's beautiful but can I tell you a secret?"

"Sure."

"When I saw the box I was hoping it was your class ring."

I knew what she was suggesting, the ring would have meant that we were going steady.

"I don't have one," I was forced to confess.

I was going to have to explain to her that I couldn't afford a class ring, when suddenly a car backed out of Mr. Fleming's house onto the traffic on Clifton Avenue.

"Look," Doris exclaimed and pulled away from me.

"Hold on," I said as I disengaged the emergency brake and put the Dodge into first gear. The gearshift was on the steering column.

It was Mr. Fleming driving a big, new, maroon Studebaker. He drove east on Clifton, toward downtown Cleveland. I tried to follow behind him without coming too close so he would not see us.

The dusk helped our cover and I hoped that he didn't look in his rearview mirror too often. From what I could see he seemed too intent with driving to notice us.

"Look, he's turning onto West Boulevard," Doris said.

I pulled hard to the port on the Ford's big steel steering wheel. He was heading toward Edgewater Beach. It was a bit too cold for a swim. I wondered why he was going there.

Edgewater Beach on Lake Erie was divided into two areas. The upper level contained picnic areas and a bathhouse, the lower area sported a long sandy beach and a couple of fishing piers.

Mr. Fleming drove past the upper area and went down the small hill by the fishing piers. He stopped in the parking area. There was only room for a handful of cars but because of the cold weather the place was empty.

Doris and I parked in the upper area for fear of being seen. We found a parking space on the edge of a cliff overlooking the beach and behind a big oak tree. We could see Mr. Fleming's car but he would have to be looking up, backwards and sideways, to see us.

We hoped he was too preoccupied with his mission to notice us. He jumped out of his car, carrying a canvas bag with him. He walked quickly toward the fishing pier.

"I wonder what he has in that bag?" Doris said what we were both thinking.

"It's getting darker and harder to see him," I said.

Mr. Fleming was carrying a large flashlight with his bag. There was a lone fisherman on the pier. I figured he was braving the cold wind in hopes of bringing some blue pike home for his family's dinner.

"Damn, we're too far away. My camera's not going to be any good. I knew I should have brought my brother's telephoto lens."

"There's not enough light, anyway," Doris added.

Mr. Fleming walked past the fisherman and appeared to drop his satchel next to him.

"He dropped his bag," Doris said.

"Yeah, and he didn't stop to pick it up."

Fleming kept walking to the end of the pier and flashed his light into the darkness. Then he turned it on and off a few times as if he was giving a signal to someone.

Suddenly another light appeared on the water.

"What's that?" Doris asked.

"Looks like a boat."

The boat flashed its light a few times back to Mr. Fleming. Then Mr. Fleming turned, walked past the fisherman, back to his car and left.

"What's going on?" I wondered.

"Fleming's leaving, we should follow him," Doris said.

"I think we should stay and watch the fisherman for a while."

Doris gave a long sigh of disapproval but deferred to my wishes. So we sat for a while and watched the fisherman. He picked up the satchel and attached a big red bobber on it. We were losing light by the minute but we could see him attach his fishing line to it and throw it in the lake.

Then the boat pulled up, grabbed the bobber and the satchel with a net and sped back out into Lake Erie. I suddenly remembered the boat that almost ran over Ed, Frank and me the previous summer in just about the same location.

"That's it," I said. "He's up to something."

"I guess you're right," Doris admitted.

"What time is it?"

She checked her wristwatch. "It's only six o'clock. It sure gets dark early now."

"Well, we still have an hour before Frank needs the car back," I said.

"Yes, a whole hour." She slid over closer to me.

I put my arm around her and smelled her perfume. She put her hand on my knee and looked up at me.

We forgot all about Mr. Fleming. And we were late bringing Frank his car back.

CHAPTER NINETEEN: The Radio Club

We had a short Christmas break that year, coming back to school before the new year started. I was sitting in *The Tatler* office on the first day of the new semester when it hit me. Mr. Friedrich had given me a stack of press releases to look through for story ideas. We called them press releases but actually they were just a bunch of memos from various teachers about the clubs that they sponsored.

I had put my investigation of Mr. Fleming on hold for the Holidays. Besides the usual family gatherings, my cousin Joe had received his draft notice. He was ordered to report to the 101st Airborne in Fort Benning, Georgia right after New Year's Day. So we tried to make his holiday as enjoyable as possible.

As soon as I returned to school I wrestled with what to do about Mr. Fleming. He was obviously up to no good. I wanted to tell someone about him but I did not know whom to trust. My parents were no help. They regarded our teachers as saints.

I considered confiding in one of our other teachers but I was unsure if I could trust any of them, even Mr. Friedrich. My homeroom teacher, Mr. Bader, had already left for the Army.

I almost wished that I had not stuck my nose into Mr. Fleming's affairs. Senior year of high school was enough of a headache without taking on the problems of the real world.

I was still debating my next course of action when I spotted a press release about West Tech's radio club. The government was forcing them to dismantle their amateur ham radio because of the war. And who was doing the dismantling?

Mr. Harold Fleming, the radio club sponsor, that's who. I remembered the big antenna on his Lake Road home. I was sure that he had a plausible explanation for it but whatever it was I was not buying it.

What were they going to do with West Tech's ham radio? Would Mr. Fleming use the parts for his own setup? Would they reassemble it at someone else's house? There was a story there. I could smell it. But I needed someone to sniff it out for me. I needed a plant in the radio club. I couldn't do it my self, Mr. Fleming would be suspicious of my sudden interest. I had to take someone into my confidence. But who? Once again, I was baffled and frustrated.

I decided to talk to Doris about it. We had spent most

of Christmas vacation together and had become "an item."

I met her for lunch in the cafeteria. We shared the same time period again for the new semester but I talked her into at least having a bite with me before heading to the library. As soon as I mentioned my idea she jumped at the opportunity.

"*I'll* do it," she said with a quickness that surprised me.

"No, I don't think that's a good idea."

"Why not?" She looked hurt.

"It might be a dangerous assignment. If Mr. Fleming catches on who knows what he might do. I need a guy to do it."

"A *guy?*" Doris' eyes flashed in anger for the first time since we'd been dating. "If my sister can work at the bomber plant I can join a school club."

"It's not that simple," I tried to appease her. We both stopped eating our sandwiches and glared into one another's eyes across the lunch table.

"You don't trust me." She looked down at her food. Tears began to form in her eyes.

"Of course, I trust you." I took her hand into mine. "If I didn't I wouldn't be talking to you about it right now. I'm just worried about you."

"You're worried about me?" she looked up slowly.

"Yes."

"That's sweet." She smiled, wiping the tears from

her eyes.

After she settled down she realized that I was not going to change my mind. So she offered a few of her friends as possible plants. But the more we talked about it the more convinced I became to not even tell her about who I sent. It would keep her out of danger.

"I'm beginning to feel that I should not have involved you," I told her.

"Why's that? You mean that from now on you don't want my help?"

"You've been a great help and I can use your advice but Mr. Fleming is starting to scare me. This could turn real nasty real quick. That's why I want to turn it over to the police."

"Then why don't you?"

"I just want a little bit more evidence so they really believe me. I'm still afraid they would tell me I'm crazy and then Mr. Fleming and Tuck would find out and my goose would be cooked."

Just then the bell rang and we had to vacate the cafeteria.

"Going to the library?" she asked me.

"No, I'm going to run down a few prospects."

She knew what I meant so she gave my hand a squeeze, picked up her books and left me standing in the midst of the cafeteria crowd. I wanted to walk her to the library but there was no time. I headed to the rec room.

Since I had already involved Frank's car in my caper it was time to let him in on my suspicions. He was one of my best friends and someone I could trust. I looked for him at his usual lunchtime haunt, dancing in the rec room.

"Seen Frank Roulette, the dancing fool?" I asked one of his friends from the aircraft shop.

"He's working on big project for Mr. Van Meter," the guy told me. "He's probably going to be working his lunch hours the rest of the semester."

Once again I put my Tatler pass to work but this was an easy move since I only had to travel a short hop through the basement.

The aircraft engine shop occupied a huge cavern at the east end of the basement, underneath the horticulture greenhouses. The engines were bolted to the floor because even though the propellers were smaller than normal they still managed to exert a powerful tugging motion. Every aircraft major had a story about an engine almost flying away on them.

When I tugged on the doorknob to enter their domain I received a slight electrical jolt. It made me jump and made my hair stand on its end. I could hear a group of students laughing inside.

When I opened the door four students looked up from one of the large engines that they were inspecting. They were all laughing at me. And Frank was one of them.

"*Et tu*, Ace?" I said.

"Just one of the ways we pass the time down here."
He shook my clean hand with his greasy one.

His friends looked like surgeons operating on a
patient in a hospital, all bunched up on top of a large airplane engine, their hands full of tools, like bees on a hive.

"Shut the door behind you," the teacher, Mr. Van
Meter, hollered at me after I entered. He was oversee-
ing the team of mechanics. "We're about to crank it up."

"Sorry sir," I said. "Might I have a word with
Frank?"

"Go ahead," he waved us away as he gave the com-
mand to start the engine. Soon the whole room was
filled with a deep-pitched roar.

"So what brings you, Slats?" Frank asked as he
guided me away from the noise.

"I was hoping you'd do me a favor, old friend."

"What's with the old friend bit? I'm not giving you
my car again and I'm not lending you any money."

Money was often a motivating factor in Frank's
decisions. He knew the value of a dollar. Or should
I say a penny.

"No, nothing like that. It's pretty simple. I need you
to join the radio club for a while."

"The radio club? What for?"

"It's hard to explain but it would be great if you could
just go to a couple meetings for me. They have one tonight
tenth period. If you could just go, keep your mouth shut

and listen I'll explain everything at my house."

"Sorry, no can do. I've got a new part-time job that I start tonight. Working at Warner-Swasey."

Warner-Swasey was a tool and die company on Cleveland's west side.

"Wow, that's the big time. How'd you get that job?"

"Mr. Van Meter lined me up. He said I was one of his best students."

"Great, that'll be some nice cash."

"You better believe it. But I can't help you with the radio club. What's that about?"

"I'll tell you later. Just keep it to yourself for now, okay?"

"My lips are sealed."

"Loose lips sink ships."

"You're kidding right?"

"No, this is serious. I have to go. We'll talk later."

"Okay, see ya Slats." Frank smacked me on the back with his big greasy hand. I was afraid what that might look like but I didn't have time to worry about it. My mind was already juggling some other possibilities. "Be careful with the door knob on the way out."

I pushed on the wood door instead of the metal knob and laughed. I would have to go to my backup plan. My cousin Paul Starzinsky was majoring in welding. The welding shop was also located in a basement classroom that I could easily reach without

Mousey catching me. The basement's subterranean culture was a bit different than the rest of the school's. A bit more on the wild side you might say.

Paul and I were not really that close. We never hung out or anything but he was family. We saw each other at all the family gatherings like on Christmas and Easter. I last saw him over Christmas break and we had talked about Tech and the war and stuff. I figured I could trust him more than most people.

I wasn't sure of his schedule. I thought I'd take a shot and try the welding room. Like Frank he might be finishing his morning gig or starting an afternoon class.

The welding room was smaller than the aircraft room but just as chaotic. Sparks were flying as the students were using their oxyacetylene torches.

I found Paul welding some steel legs to the bottom of a sheet metal table. I did not see his teacher. He must have gone to the bathroom or to the cafeteria for a quick lunch.

The metal table that Paul was welding was placed upside down on a wooden workbench. He was wearing special dark goggles to protect his eyes from the bright light of the torch. I was almost afraid to interrupt him. If I surprised him and he moved the torch too quickly he could cut his arm off with the flame even though he was wearing heavy-duty industrial protective clothing.

So I moved into his line of vision, holding my hand over my eyes to protect them from the flying sparks. I tried not to look at the flame. It was so bright it could damage my eyes just looking at it.

"Paul," I hollered at him.

He looked up, spotted me, then lifted his goggles. "Hey cuz, what are you doing here? Is everything okay?"

I guessed that he thought there was a problem with one of our family members. "No, nothing like that. Can I talk to you a second?"

"It's not a great time," he held up his torch with one hand to emphasize his point.

"I know but it's important."

"Okay," he reached over and turned off two knobs, one on the top of each canister. One tank held oxygen, the other acetylene. The flame disappeared.

"What are you working on?"

"Tables for the Army. What's going on?"

"I need your help and it might be more important than those tables for the Army."

"Are you in some sort of trouble?"

"No, but I need someone I can trust. Can we talk in private?"

"Come on back to the clean-up room, no one should be in there until class is over."

The welding room had its own lavatory with a large circular washbasin. A large metal ring on the floor circled around it that you put your foot on to make the water squirt out. Paul grabbed a bunch of white goop from a can on top of the basin and began washing his hands.

"Sorry to interrupt your project."

"No big deal, I was almost done for the day. What's the matter?"

"I need someone to go to the radio club meeting for me tonight. I know it's short notice. It's tenth period after school."

"That's it? What's the big deal?"

"Well, you can't let them know you're going there for me. That's why I need someone I can trust, and you're family."

"Top secret, huh? What's the catch?"

I looked around the lavatory. Someone could walk in at any time to use the facilities. "This isn't a good place to talk. Could you just go like you wanted to join and we could talk about it later?"

"I guess. Is this for a story for *The Tatler*?"

"Something like that. You can't let on that I asked you, okay? I'll owe you big time."

"I've got some time after school. I could meet you back at your house."

"That would be great."

"You know what would really be great?" he said. "How about if your mom made me some of her cheese-cake? I don't know why but my mom never learned to cook like yours."

I did not know why his mom had trouble in the cooking department. Maybe it was just her temperament but I had an alternative theory. The two women were sisters. My mom was the oldest child, his was the youngest. Maybe by the time my aunt Melba came along their mom, our grandmother, was too burned out to teach her anything. Life was rough on women back then.

"You got it," I told him. "Just pretend you're interested in joining. You know, it's senior year and you always wanted to join but never had the time and it's your last chance. Something like that. But you don't even know me."

"Good thing we have different last names."

"Good thing."

It was a done deal. I just hoped that I was not putting my cousin Paul in harm's way. I hurried back to the rec room, wondering what my next move should be.

CHAPTER TWENTY:
The Cheesecake Caper

Paul came over to my house on West 47th St. right after his radio club meeting. I was feeding my brother Johnny's pigeons. It was difficult for him to take care of them in the winter. He had trouble navigating the ice and snow with his crutches so I helped him out. Besides, it was good background for my *Argosy* story about him.

The pigeons were kept in a big cage inside the garage. Johnny had drilled a hole in one of the concrete block walls for them to fly in and out. My other brother, Andy, had built the garage out of the blocks because he needed a place to park his 1935 Ford Roadster while he went off to the Army. He was the first one to own a car in our family and no one else was even allowed to touch it.

"Hello, Victor." Paul surprised me as I was dishing out birdseed.

"Hey Paul, how'd it go? I didn't see you come up."

"It was different," he said with a smile. "I can see why you're interested in those guys."

"You can?"

"Hey, I wasn't born yesterday. There's something not quite right with the radio club."

"What makes you say that?" I finished feeding the pigeons and motioned to Paul that we could sit on one of the wooden chairs that were stored in the garage for the winter.

"I told them I wanted to join their club but I could tell that they wanted no part of me."

"What'd they say?"

"They kept saying that the government was closing down their call letters because of the war and they were putting the equipment in mothballs."

"What about Mr. Fleming? What'd he say?"

"He was the worst. He practically insisted that the club was disbanding and it was useless for any new members to join."

"Ah, they didn't want you. That tells me a lot."

"About what?"

"It's probably better you don't know. I think they are up to something but I can't prove it."

"You want me to go to the next meeting?"

"No, you've done enough. I don't think they'll tell you anything."

"You going to write a story about them for *The Tatler*?"

"No, keep it quiet for now, okay? I'm not sure what I'm getting myself into. It might be dangerous."

"What do think, I'm afraid of a bunch of krauts? Those guys don't scare me."

"What'd you mean 'a bunch of krauts'?"

"You didn't know? They're all a bunch of Germans. They were even talking in German before I showed up."

"They were?"

"Yeah, they were sure surprised to see me. At first I thought they didn't want me to join because I'm Irish-Russian. My parents hate the Germans from the last war."

"You might be right."

"Anyhow, how's your brother Johnny doing these days? You helping him with his pigeons?"

"Yeah, you want a couple? They're getting to be too much for him."

"Not me, I've got a hunting dog. We don't feed birds. We shoot 'em. Pheasants and ducks."

'You want to come inside and warm up?"

"No thanks, got to run. My mom's waiting dinner on me."

"Wait a minute, I forgot, I've got something for you."

I ran inside the house while Paul checked out the pigeons. I returned with a special order of my mom's cheesecake. I had asked her to bake one for Paul when I came home from school. But it wasn't the kind of cheesecake we eat today that is made out of cream cheese. It was more like a big round loaf of homemade sweet bread with a couple inches of melted cheddar cheese piled on top. I always said that you could live a couple days off a loaf of my mother's cheesecake.

"Here you go, hot out of the oven, I didn't expect you so soon."

"That's why I came over right away," Paul smiled as he opened the top of the brown paper sack and took a long smell. "I did remember one more thing while you were inside."

"What's that?"

"They're having a New Year's Eve party at the Haufbrau House. I guess I'm not invited."

"The Haufbrau House, isn't that on the east side?"

"Yeah, they said a bunch of Tech kids are playing in the band. Let me know if you need any more help. I didn't like those guys."

"Neither do I. Thanks for the offer."

I waved him good-bye. He only lived a few blocks away. I knew the cheesecake would still be warm when he got home. I was already planning my next move, New Year's Eve.

CHAPTER TWENTY-ONE
New Year's Eve

New Year's Eve, 1941. World War II had just started. It was my final semester at Tech and I did not know what to do about Mr. Fleming. What a way to break in 1942. I was a bit scared of the future. And fear was an emotion that was new to me. Thankfully, I was too busy to worry much about it.

I discovered that I knew one of the guys playing in the band at the Haufbrau House. So I invited Doris to break in the New Year with me and do a little spying on the side. Maybe I could discover some clue as to what Mr. Fleming was plotting. If I could only discover his plans for the blueprints in his office I'd have enough evidence to go to the authorities.

But once again I had car problems. I did not have one. My only course of action was a bit dangerous. I was going to have to steal one. Fortunately, it was going to be my brother Andy's 1935 Ford Roadster. The upside was that if I was caught I probably would not go to prison. The downside was that my mother would make my life a living hell and my brother would try to kill me when he came back home.

I was not too wild about taking Andy's car to the east side. The east side had a reputation as the more dangerous side of town. What would I do if it was stolen or damaged? I'd probably have to commit hara-kiri.

I asked Doris to join me. Despite my concern over her safety I had to have a date. And I wasn't about to let anyone else take her out on New Year's Eve. I didn't tell her about the German Club. Instead I told her we were going to see my friend Dennis Plezak play with his band, The Pioneers.

Doris looked beautiful when I picked her up. Her long hair was arranged on top of her head in a new look for the New Year. Her dress was full length and sleeveless. Her legs were covered but her arms looked lean and sexy. I realized that I had not seen her arms all winter.

We made small talk as I drove along the Shoreway, the highway that bordered Lake Erie. It was the first time that I had ventured further east than downtown Cleveland. Fortunately the Haufbrau House was right off the Shoreway exit so I did not worry about losing my way.

Once we stepped out of my brother's car the cold wind off the lake flung bits of snow at our faces like rice at a wedding. I was already worried about the drive back.

"Maybe we should have stayed closer to home," I said to Doris as we lowered our heads into the elements.

"No, this is fun. I've never been here before."

Entering the warm Hofbrau House relaxed all our senses. It smelled like my mom's kitchen and the layout reminded me of the West Tech cafeteria. There were big pans full of eastern European ethnic food and it was served buffet-style.

The band was playing some German oom-pa-pa song against the back wall right next to a fireplace. Couples were dancing the polka in front of the band, laughing and singing the lyrics along with the lead singer.

"Let's say hi to my buddy Dennis," I told Doris as we gave our coats to the hatcheck girl.

"Fine," she agreed.

We wormed our way through the New Year's revelers.

"Nice gig," I yelled to Dennis as he was squeezing his accordion.

"Catch you at the break," he hollered back.

All six band members were from Tech. I wondered which one was Mr. Fleming's connection. Dennis told me earlier that Mr. Maricic, the school's band instructor, had booked them with the Haufbrau House. Any paying gig was a great opportunity for a group of high school musicians. Not only did they sound good, they also seemed to know all the traditional ethnic music that the dancers remembered from their home countries, like the polkas and waltzes.

"Doris, would you like to dance?" I asked her.

"Of course. We've never danced before."

"I'm not too good at this polka stuff. I only know a little bit from family weddings."

"Me too," she shouted above the music.

We bounced around the dance floor in a wide circle, trying to imitate the older crowd. The polka is a fun dance, it makes you laugh and is a workout. We did two numbers in a row and then the band announced a break, which was fortunate for me because I was winded.

"Geez, that works up your appetite," I exclaimed.

"No kidding. Should we get something to eat?"

"Let's find Dennis."

Dennis was putting his accordion back into its case when we approached him.

"Man, you were really working that thing." I told him.

"You betcha. What brings you to the east side for the big holiday?"

"We heard there was a hot band playing here tonight." I laughed. "Do you know Doris?"

"Yeah, we had an English class together."

"You didn't tell me that," I said to Doris.

"I'm sorry, I forgot until I saw him." She shook Dennis' hand.

"Victor, Doris, you recognize the guys?" Dennis turned and waved his hand in front of the group.

"Sure," I lied. I recognized their faces but did not know their names. They all said hello but seemed more in a hurry to hit the bathroom and grab some chow than exchange pleasantries.

"Like to join us for some grub?" I asked Dennis.

"After I make a stop in the men's room," he said as delicately as possible in deference to Doris.

We parted ways and took a place in the buffet line. It was unusually long because of the band break. As we waited I finally took the time to check out the customers.

It did not take long to spot Siegfried Walsh from Tech's football team. I remembered him from the first time I visited Mr. Fleming's room after school and our dispute in the cafeteria. He was sitting at a table with another group of familiar faces. Just like with the band, I recognized many of them but did not know most of their names.

I figured Siegfried was sitting with the radio club. My cousin Paul was correct. They did have a similar look about them, mostly blondes with blue eyes, what you expected from our German population. And large glasses of beer were strewn around the table.

Drinking beer at a young age was a custom in the old country but I doubted if any of them were old enough by America's standards. The Hofbrau House had a reputation for looking the other way in such matters.

I gave the radio club the quick once over then looked the other way. I was trying to appear inconspicuous when my eyes traveled to the front of the food line.

There was Mr. Fleming piling some wiener schnitzel on his plate. He was joking with the middle-aged lady working behind the big hot pans of food. They were talking in German. My two semesters of German class helped me little in understanding them. To learn a language you had to use it and the only foreign language in my home were my parents speaking Russian to each other.

"Look who's here," I nudged Doris and nodded my head in Mr. Fleming's direction.

She looked at him and nodded back but with a timidity that I had never seen in her before. It was almost as if she was afraid of him. I tried not to let it bother me but it did. Maybe it was a mistake to bring her along after all.

I watched as the waitress poured lager beer into a huge stein for Mr. Fleming. He took his tray and joined the radio club at their table. I looked away again and suddenly felt a stab of fear in my heart.

What the heck was I doing here? What did I expect to accomplish? There was whole table of Tech students who would turn on me in an instant if they knew I was spying on them. And here I am with a female accomplice that I would have to protect if things turned rough.

Suddenly the sweet smells of the German food made my stomach upset. I steered Doris to a table as far away as possible from the radio club.

Dennis found us and sat down. "What do you think, Slats? How do we sound?"

"Great, why don't you tell Doris how you learned all that old-fashioned stuff. I have to use the men's room myself."

"I can tell you in one word, weddings," Dennis laughed. "Make that two words. Cash is the other one."

I laughed with them and excused myself. Dennis looked as if he enjoyed entertaining Doris.

I found the rest room and went directly to a stall to sit in. My upset stomach was more mental than physical but I needed a bit of quiet to decide my next move. What did I get myself into? What was I going to say to Mr. Fleming? I should have planned this better. What was the old saying about fools rushing in?

As I pondered my situation with my pants down around my knees I heard a couple boys come in talking loudly, as if they had been drinking. They were emptying their bladders standing in front of the urinals.

"What's Doris doing here?" one of them asked angrily. "Does Mr. Fleming know about it?"

The knot in my stomach tightened.

"Don't worry, he'll have a full report Monday morning," the other boy laughed. "Herr Fleming has everything under control."

"What about the bomber plant? It's a new year and we still have not done anything about it."

I suddenly felt like throwing up but remained very quiet for fear of being discovered.

"All in due time, my comrade, all in due time."

"Well, I say we blow the place up before they build any more planes to bomb our fatherland."

"You talk tough, Edwin, but it is easier said than done."

Then they washed their hands like they had learned in West Tech's health class and went out the door. I tried to stand up but my knees buckled. I felt like they had been cut out from under me.

I sat back down and tried to think about what had just occurred. My mind was twirling around so fast it made me dizzy. I tried to compose myself. I waited in the rest room for a few minutes so the guys who just left could not guess that I was in there with them. But more customers came in and I looked foolish hanging around the bathroom. I took my time washing my hands and looked at my face in the mirror. Suddenly my fear turned into anger. I had been taken for a ride. I wanted revenge, not just on the German guys, but also on Doris. I walked back into the restaurant and lost myself in the crowd.

The noise, the dancing, the food, the music, they were attacking all my senses at the same time. I did not know how to react to all of it so I just let my instincts take over.

"Where you been, man?" Dennis asked. "I thought you fell in the toilet."

"Sorry buddy, I don't feel so good," I plopped down in my seat like a broken man.

"What? Too much sauerkraut?" he laughed. He bid Doris good-bye and went back to his accordion.

"Are you all right?" she asked me.

"Not really, I think I'm coming down with something." I could not look her in the eyes. "How's your food?"

"Great," she said. "Do you want to go home?" She seemed almost as eager as I was to leave.

"Finish your plate first, I hate to ruin your evening."

"No, I don't mind, really. Just the trip out here was enough for me."

"Well, if you don't mind, my stomach does feel terrible."

"You must have picked up a bug," she smiled. I almost fell for it. I helped her up from her chair and we headed toward the coat checkroom. Out of the corner of my eye I saw Mr. Fleming stand up and walk toward us.

I tried hurrying Doris to the door but he intercepted us just as the band began to play again.

"Victor Blazek, I thought I saw you here earlier. What brings you so far from home?"

"I know the band," I said as I gave the hat check

lady our ticket and a small tip.

"Oh yes," he sounded a bit drunk. "Another example of West Tech's superior education. Your friend looks familiar."

"I thought you two might know each other," I said with just a hint of sarcasm as I helped Doris put her coat on. I could not help myself. "Doris Fidelmeister, I'm sure you've heard of Mr. Harold Fleming, our famous chemistry teacher.

"Pleased to meet you." She put out her hand to shake his but he took it and kissed it. He was too drunk to notice her cringe but I did and suddenly I changed my mind about Doris. Maybe she was trapped in something that I did not understand.

"We were just leaving," I interrupted them and it felt good. I took Doris' arm and led her toward the door but Mr. Fleming blocked our path.

"You're not going to ring in the New Year with us?" he said with a wink. "This place is so much fun."

"I have to take my brother's car back," I said matter-of-factly.

"Well, do be careful driving home," he gave Doris a sly smile. "The road conditions are terrible."

"I know how to drive in the snow. See you back at Tech."

"Good evening," he held the door open for us. The cold air felt as icy as Mr. Fleming's demeanor. It instantly brought me to my senses.

I could feel Mr. Fleming's stare as we walked out into the parking lot. I looked back at the restaurant door. He was still watching us. Something about his facial expression made me feel uncomfortable but I didn't say anything to Doris about it.

CHAPTER TWENTY-TWO:
The Ride Home

Before Doris and I could leave the Haufbrau House parking lot I had to scrape the snow off the windows of my brother's car. I could not find a scraper anywhere so I had to use my gloves. Doris sat inside as the car warmed up and I did my best to clear the windows. I was using the time to think about how I should approach Doris about Mr. Fleming. But it was too cold for contemplation. I jumped inside the warm car before I could come up with an effective strategy.

The front window's border was still covered with ice and the windshield wipers barely cleared the open area. My visibility was greatly impaired. As we exited toward the side street I did not see another car that was leaving the parking lot at the same time.

"Look out," Doris said.

"Oops." When I hit the brakes the big Ford slid on the ice.

But the other car did not pull out of the way.

Instead it waited for me to leave first.

"Why aren't they moving?" I asked Doris as I peered through the icy windshield.

"I guess they don't trust your driving," she laughed. "Mister don't worry, I can drive in the snow."

I laughed with her and felt good about our relationship again. I decided the ride home was the wrong time to talk about her and Mr. Fleming.

We drove north on East 55th street and jumped back onto the Shoreway. I noticed the other car was following us. I figured it was just another couple also heading back to the west side.

But they stayed right behind us and I hated that. I was taking my time with my brother's car and wasn't about to speed, especially on the icy pavement. After driving for a few minutes with their lights filling up my mirror, I finally slowed down and pulled over so they could pass us.

"What's with that car? It won't get off my tail."

"Just wait and let them pass," Doris said.

"I am." And I did. But they still did not pass.

So I sped up again and so did they. Finally they pulled up next to me. I thought they were going to be on their way so I tried to see who they were. But my side window was too fogged up.

Then suddenly, for no apparent reason, instead of just passing us they tried to force us off the road. We were on a section of the Shoreway next to an electric plant that sucks in water from Lake Erie. We were driving over the inlet where only a metal barrier separated the road from the lake.

The other car began knocking into my brother's Roadster, trying to push us into Lake Erie.

"What's going on?" Doris screamed.

"I don't know," I hollered back.

"It's Fleming's boys," Doris said. "They're trying to kill us."

I could not continue as I was for very long. Doris and I would end up swimming in Lake Erie. And we would not last very long in the cold water. It was time for a change of tactics, my brother's car be damned.

"What are you doing?" Doris asked as I slammed on the brakes and began to skid on the ice just as they were attempting to slam into us again.

Their car sped past us. They tried to stop to let us catch up to them but they spun in front of us and I hit them broadside. Doris screamed but I put my foot on the gas and hit them hard. There were no seat belts back then so Doris's head hit the dashboard as we crashed into the other car. I looked over at her. She fell back in the seat unconscious. I was pushing the other car sideways. I didn't know what to do next.

Then I saw the other driver. It was Seigfried Walsh, my arch enemy. Our eyes met for a brief second. His were full of hatred, mine full of anger. I lost my temper and punched the accelerator again. My brother's bumper slid along the side of their car until suddenly their car was on Doris' side of us going in the wrong direction. I saw Siegfried's partner, sitting in the passenger seat, shaking his fist at me as their car scraped the side of ours, knocking off the passenger side mirror.

Then they were gone, lost in the blizzard behind us. The snow was falling and it was hard to see in my mirror. Then I saw their car go head first into another car.

There was a fiery crash. I was tempted to stop and help but I looked over at Doris and decided to hell with them. I had to take Doris to the hospital and do it in a hurry.

CHAPTER TWENTY-THREE: The Hospital

I had to think quickly. Where was the closest hospital? The nearest one I could remember was Lutheran Hospital by the West Side Market. It was near downtown and right off the Shoreway. I remembered it because it was where my father had his appendix removed. I had visited him there as a young boy.

I looked over at Doris slumped against the door. She was unconscious. What had I done to her? If it was anything serious I would never be able to forgive myself. I drove as fast as I could but I had to be careful not to have another accident.

It seemed to take forever to find Lutheran Hospital. I pulled straight into the emergency area and a couple attendants scooped her up, put her on a gurney and took her inside.

I parked my brother's car in the hospital lot. There were dents and scrapes all over it. Andy was going to kill me if Mr. Fleming did not do it first. I would have to deal with both of them later. Doris was my main concern. Back inside the hospital a nurse showed me to her room. The doctor asked me what happened.

There was already a bandage holding a bag of ice on her forehead.

"We had an accident," I explained. "I could barely see outside so I was not paying attention to her. I think she hit her head on the dashboard."

"Ah yes, we have had a number of them tonight," the doctor said very efficiently and with a touch of a foreign accent. "She has a lump on her forehead but otherwise she seems fine. She should recover quickly."

"Thank you, doctor, that is great news," I said. I walked over closer to Doris and held her hand.

"Are you her husband?" he asked me.

"No, just her boyfriend," I heard myself saying and immediately wondered what it would be like to be married to Doris.

The doctor told me to keep the cold compress on her bump. Then he left us alone. A nurse came by and asked me if I needed anything and I said 'no.' I just looked down at Doris' sweet, innocent face and wondered what kind of a hold Mr. Fleming had on her.

It did not take me long to find out. Much to my surprise Doris came out of her state of shock rather quickly.

"Where am I?" she asked.

"Lutheran Hospital," I told her. "You hit your

head on the dashboard."

"Could I have a drink of water?"

I poured her one from a nearby pitcher. "The doctor says you are going to be all right."

She took a long drink of water with a straw.

"What happened to those boys who were trying to smash us? Why were they doing that?"

"Maybe you should tell me," I said softly.

She looked me directly in my eyes and tears began to flow from hers. "You know, don't you?"

"Yes, I know. How could you do that to me?"

"You do not know Mr. Fleming like I know him," she sobbed. "He is a very mean man. And a very powerful one."

"What did he do to you?"

"Nothing to me, at least not yet, not until he finds out that you know about me. But his power stretches back to our homeland. He will have my grandparents killed unless I do as he says."

"What does he want you to do?"

"Just find out what you know about him and keep him informed. He knew you were on to him from the beginning."

"Sheez, I never suspected anything. How could I be so stupid?"

"You weren't stupid, you were in love with me." She took my hand and gently rubbed it with both of hers.

I used my other hand to clasp hands with her. I did not know what to say to her.

"Victor," she said quietly and I leaned down to hear her better. "I did not tell him that we saw him dropping messages in the water at Edgewater. You cannot let him know that I was there. If he finds out he will kill my grandparents. I know he will."

She began to sob uncontrollably. I put my arms around her and hugged her tightly. "We have to call your parents," I said.

"Yes, you had better."

"Don't worry, I won't tell anyone that you were at Edgewater with me."

"Thank you. Thank you. Thank you."

"You don't have to thank me for anything. You were a big help."

"No I wasn't. I was terrible. Just tell me that you love me."

"I love you," I said. And I really meant it.

CHAPTER TWENTY FOUR: The NEA Building

The first Monday of the new year the auto crash killing two Tech students was the talk of the school. I was worried all weekend that a witness would tie Doris and me to the accident, but no one came forward. There were stories about it in all three of Cleveland's daily newspapers.

The scenario was identical in each one. Siegfried Walsh and Hans Guttemar, both members of the West Tech radio club, had lost control of their car on the icy Shoreway and hit the other vehicle. It was a tragic accident but blameless. And there were no witnesses left alive from either vehicle to dispute the facts. I was unsure if even Mr. Fleming knew the truth.

I had snuck my brother Andy's car into our garage sight unseen. I fed my brother Johnny's pigeons in the morning before going to school to buy some time. Johnny did not like venturing outside in the winter unless it was absolutely necessary. And my sisters seldom visited the garage in the cold months either. I hoped to wait a day or two until things cooled down and then take the Roadster to my friends in Tech's auto shop. I was sure they could fix it up for me, maybe as a class project. They often fixed cars for the teachers or students at little or no cost.

I was still too confused to know what to do or whom to trust. I went to my classes as if I was walking in my sleep. I roamed through the halls between classes looking over my shoulder, wondering if Mr. Fleming was watching me.

What was his next move going to be? What should I do? Should I go on the offensive or plan a solid defense? I was thinking on my feet the way I had learned in wrestling for the past two years. In a wrestling match you had to make split second decisions based on your opponent's actions. And you hoped your body was able to follow your brain's instructions.

I felt a sense of relief as I walked into *The Tatler* office ninth period. I had made it through the day unscathed. There were no incidents to report. I had not run into Mr. Fleming. And for some reason Maria looked dazzling.

I always felt at home working on *The Tatler*. There was a relaxed, casual atmosphere in Mr. Friedrich's classroom that was missing in most of my other discipline-oriented classes.

However, my peace of mind did not last very long.

"Victor," Mr. Friedrich addressed me before I could even find a desk to stretch out in. "I need you to do me a favor. To do the school a favor."

"What's that?" I asked, approaching his desk.

"We need you to run *The Tatler* copy down to the NEA building."

"What *Tatler* copy? What's the NEA building?"

"The NEA is the Newspaper Enterprise Association. It's where *The Tatler* is printed."

My mind was reeling. How come I did not know that?

"But *The Tatler* doesn't come out for a couple weeks," I said.

"Principal Tuck already put together a special one page edition about the New Year's Eve car crash. We need you to run the galley sheet downtown."

"Why me?" I was worried that Tuck might know about my role in the car crash.

"We have a regular courier but he's not scheduled for today. Mr. Tuck asked me for someone he could trust with such an important task and I suggested you. It's a bit of an honor and I am sure the principal will remember the favor."

"What if I can't do it?"

"I guess we can find someone else," Mr. Friedrich looked crestfallen. "But this is a great opportunity for you, Victor."

I thought about it for a few seconds. I figured Mr. Friedrich would be disappointed after sticking his neck out for me. "Mr. Tuck wants *The Tatler* out right away?"

"Tomorrow."

"Tomorrow? That's crazy."

"Mr. Tuck was not too happy that two of his students were killed and the story was splattered on the front page of the newspapers."

"He was mad?"

"He was furious. The principal does not like his school being shown in a bad light. He wants to stop any rumors before they begin."

"Rumors?"

"You know how kids are, by the end of the day there will be all kinds of wild rumors flying around the hallways. Principal Tuck wants to put out the official word and *The Tatler* is the ideal vehicle for it."

"Okay, I'll do it for you Mr. Friedrich, but I have to tell you that you're putting me on the spot."

"I am? Why's that?"

"I can't tell you right now. Maybe I should, but I can't."

Mr. Friedrich looked confused for the first time since I had known him. "Well, when you feel that you can tell me, please don't hesitate. You're one of my finest students, Victor."

The compliment did little to ease my fears.

"Where am I going? Can I leave now?"

"The NEA building is on West Sixth Street downtown. You can take the streetcar. But first you have to pick up the galley sheet in the print shop and an illustration at the art department." Mr. Friedrich handed me our regular hall pass and said good luck. "Bring back the hall pass before you leave. I want to make sure you have everything."

Suddenly something smelled rotten in Denmark. There was something about the way he asked me to return that made me feel like I was being set up again. Once again I questioned Mr. Friedrich's loyalty and his German roots. Could Mr. Fleming own him like he did Doris? But it was too late. I was stuck. I should have followed my original instincts and passed the task off to another student.

I hoped that Mr. Fleming did not yet know that Doris had blown his cover. She was still at home recovering from her injury. Did she become afraid and call Mr. Fleming? I needed to force him to tip his hand and I needed to do it in a hurry. Time was running out.

I was walking and thinking so fast that I walked right past Mousey.

"Mr. Blazek, your hall pass, please."

I held it up for her to see and started up the steps by her post. It was the only stairway that went from the third to the fourth floor and I was in a hurry.

"That stairway is down only, Mister Blazek."

Mousey jumped out of her seat.

Not only was I going up the wrong stairway but I was also bouncing up every other step. There was no running in the halls of West Tech and I was pushing the envelope.

"I'm going to report you to the principal, Mister Blazek," she hollered up the steps.

I just waved her off but I could tell that she was steaming. She was not used to being treated with disrespect by a lowly student. I knew I would have to pay for it later but I hoped that if she really went crying to Mr. Tuck that he would put two and two together and realize that I was on his own personal assignment. My little war with Mousey was heating up at the wrong time. There were bigger fish to fry.

West Tech's printing press was on the fourth floor. The fourth floor was not a full floor. Besides the printing press room there was the practice room for the band, a storage area for the band's instruments and a couple empty offices. One of the offices was used by the radio club.

The printing press room was a working print shop. The students printed much of what the school needed to function, like programs for the school plays and tickets for graduation. It even did work for the Cleveland Board of Education. It was one more reason that Tech was a microcosm of the larger society.

The classroom door was open because it was quite warm inside, thanks both to its top floor location and the workings of the printing presses. The teacher had stepped out so I was greeted by a couple of students wearing ink-stained T-shirts.

"Can I help you?" asked a short, greasy-haired kid who I did not know. He was purposely blocking my entrance to the shop.

"I'm here to see Mr. Dimitri."

"He stepped out, you'll have to come back later," he ordered me in a tone that I did not appreciate.

"No can do, buddy. I'm supposed to pick up a galley sheet for *The Tatler*."

"Don't know from no galley sheet," he said emphatically and tried closing the door on me.

I was about to drop Tuck's name on the kid when I saw Richard Ironjaw, another member of the wrestling team, standing around with a bunch of kids behind the counter. His name tipped off that he was of American Indian descent.

"Hey Cochise," I hollered over the short guy's head, holding the door open with my shoulder. "Can I talk to you a minute?"

"Hello, Slats," Rich said over the short guy's head. "Let him in, Shorty, he's all right."

I did not understand what all the fuss was about until I saw that most of the class was circled around a printing wheel. They were spinning it like a roulette wheel and betting pennies on what letter the little steel ball would land on.

"What's going on?"

"While the cat's away the mice must play," Ironjaw laughed. "What brings you way the heck up here?"

"I'm supposed to pick up a *Tatler* galley sheet for Mr. Friedrich," I told him while watching the ball spin around.

"I'll take a look on Mr. Dimitri's desk," Rich said. "Jump in if you want."

I took a penny out of my pocket and put it on the letter V. The letters were made out of metal, raised up from the wheel. It was called "cold type." The printers would arrange the letters on a page, cover them with ink and then run a paper over them. The process was not much different than what Ben Franklin did in colonial times.

The short guy spun the wheel and all the students cheered for their letter like they were at the racetrack. The V hit and I collected 23 pennies for my effort. It doubled the amount of money I carried in my pocket.

"Way to go, Slats," Rich said. "It's your lucky day."

"I hope so. Did you find it?"

He handed me a large manila envelope. "I think this is what you're looking for."

The envelope said TATLER on the outside. I

opened it up and saw one page of sample paper in Times New Roman typeface, the same kind we used for the paper.

"Yeah, this must be it," I said to Rich. "Thanks."

"Want to try another penny?"

"No thanks, I'll quit while I'm ahead."

Ironjaw escorted me out of his classroom. I walked down the steps to the third floor and knocked on Mr. Livingston's door. He was the art teacher. His wife was also an art teacher and they taught in adjoining rooms.

The West Tech art department was recognized in the local art world as better than most college programs. Students were trained in the classical manner. Life drawing was encouraged and the Livingstons often used live models for the students to draw.

Mrs. Livingston answered my knock. She was in her 30s, quite ravishing and bit younger than Mr. Livingston. Many of Tech's male students had a crush on her, including me.

"Eh, Mrs. Livingston, sorry to disturb you," I said. It was the first time I had ever talked to her.

"No problem," she said and stepped out into the hallway, closing the door behind her. "What can I do for you?"

"I'm Victor Blazek from *The Tatler*. Mr. Livingston is supposed to have an illustration by Bruce Eberling for a special edition." I held out my hand to shake hers. I was not sure if that was the right thing to do but she took it and gently touched it. I felt a tingle go down my spine.

"Oh yes, I know just where that is," she said. "Please wait here so we don't disturb our young artists."

She left the door slightly ajar so I could see inside the art room. A group of students with pencils in hand were hunched over their sketchbooks as they crowded around another student sitting on a chair on top of a table. He was wearing a white T-shirt, his elbow was on his knee and his head rested on his fist, a variation of Rodin's famous "The Thinker."

I saw my friend Ray Browning hard at work but he did not see me. He was too intent on his drawing. Ray was going to do the illustration for my *Argosy* story about homing pigeons. But that whole project was on a back burner. My problems with Mr. Fleming were beginning to impact my studies.

Mrs. Livingston returned with the illustration. I took a quick look at it. A policeman was inspecting a mangled car, filling out an accident report in his notebook. Meanwhile two youths were hovering above the car with wings attached to their bodies. One of them was tapping the policeman on his shoulder but he did not see them.

"Tell the kids at Tech we're sorry to miss graduation," was the caption.

The pencil drawing was exquisite. Eberling was the same student who drew *The Tatler*'s editorial cartoons.

"Nice job," I said.

"He's good," Mrs. Livingston said. "But the subject is very sad."

"I know." I wanted to give her a hug but resisted. "Tell Mr. Livingston thanks."

"I will," she squeezed my arm, turned from me and went back inside.

I felt uplifted from finally meeting Mrs. Livingston but I had to be on with my task. Mr. Friedrich was waiting for me when I returned to *The Tatler* office. He checked out the galley sheet and the illustration, said everything was in order, gave me a dollar for carfare and a bite to eat and sent me on my way.

Maybe I was wrong about him, I thought.

I took the Detroit Road trolley downtown. Detroit Road changed to Superior Avenue on the other side of the Cuyahoga River. The river divides Cleveland into two cities, the east side and the west side. The High Level Bridge over the river that connected the two sides was an amazing piece of engineering.

Street level was for automobiles going downtown. A second level ran underneath it that carried the trolleys. I looked out my window before the trolley went inside the bridge. I could see the large collection of industrial buildings and smokestacks on the banks of the Cuyahoga River, stretching as far as the eye could see.

Cleveland's factories were America's first line of defense in World War II. Its industrial capacity was the backbone of our country's response to our German and Japanese enemies. These were the same industries that Mr. Fleming was trying to destroy. I could not prove it but I could feel it in my bones.

I jumped off the trolley on West Sixth Street, just a few blocks north of the Terminal Tower. The Terminal Tower was the largest building in the world outside of New York City. Its shadow loomed large across the city's landscape. As I walked down West Sixth Street I could not shake a feeling of dread. Something did not feel right about my assignment.

It was a cold sunless afternoon that was already turning into darkness. The large gray clouds blowing off Lake Erie, pregnant with moisture, were about to cover the city with another layer of snow.

I stuck the large *Tatler* envelope under my coat so the bitter wind coming off the lake would not rip it out of my hands. I kept looking up at the various buildings, a hodgepodge of architectural styles, mostly square warehouses. Finally a yellow stone marker over a doorway proclaimed the NEA building. It was a six-story red brick structure nestled in between two similar red brick buildings.

The first thing I noticed walking inside the door of the NEA building was the smell. The aroma was the sweet smell of printer's ink. It reminded me of West Tech's greenhouse except instead of smelling rows of roses you smelled tons of newsprint.

Then there was the noise. It was overwhelming. Huge printing presses two stories tall were whirling and spinning. Different machine parts were smashing into each other as paper spun through the various cylinders. It made Tech's printing press look like a toy model.

I roamed around the place, amazed by the facility. No one paid any attention to me until a burly guy with a sleeveless T-shirt grabbed me by my collar. His ink stains matched the ones my West Tech classmates sported. He had half a cigarette perched behind his ear and a pack of Lucky Strikes shoved inside his belt.

"Hey kid, whadda ya need?" he hollered at me over the din.

"I've got a special edition of my high school paper, *The Tatler*. I'm supposed to give it to a Mr. Vail."

"From West Tech, huh? Me too," he put his big arms around my shoulders.

"Really?"

"How do you think I got this job?" he winked at me. "I still read *The Tatler* when it comes off the presses."

"You're kidding me."

"Don't believe it, I'll prove it to you. What's your name, kid?"

"Victor Blazek."

"Victor, eh? Let me see." He took his cigarette

from behind his ear, lit it and blew out a puff of smoke. "The sports writer, right?"

"Damn," I said in disbelief.

He smiled and I felt famous for a minute. He steered me to a stairway leading to a second floor office with a lot of windows overlooking the presses. "They're waiting for ya up there, kid."

"What's that?" I did not understand what he was talking about.

"Go on up, you'll be all right." He almost pushed me up the stairway.

"What did he mean by 'they'?" I thought to myself as I climbed the stairs. The steps were cast iron and shaky. They reminded me of a fire escape except they were inside the building.

I knocked on the office door but it was so loud no one answered. I opened it myself and walked in. There were three men wearing white shirts and ties sitting around a round wooden table drinking what looked like a bottle of whiskey.

"Mr. Vail?" I asked, looking from face to face. One of the men looked vaguely familiar but I could not place him.

"Yes?" the one sitting in the middle stood up. He was tall and skinny and his hands were stained with ink.

"I'm Victor Blazek from West Tech." I handed him the envelope.

Mr. Vail looked inside, pulled out the galley sheet

and illustration and laid them down on the table. "Very good, very good," he said. "Too bad about those boys."

I just nodded in agreement. For some reason I wanted to run back down the stairs. The way the other two men looked at me scared me. I sensed that they knew I was involved in the accident.

"If that's all you need," I said and turned to leave.

"There's just one more thing, Victor," the one who looked familiar said to me. "Would you mind sitting down with us for a few minutes?" He pulled out a chair across from theirs for me to sit on.

"I'd rather stand."

"Please, sit down Victor," he took my elbow and eased me toward the empty chair. "We don't bite. Mr. Vail could you give us a few moments?"

"Sure thing, Mr. Ness," Mr. Vail said, and walked out to the pressroom.

Suddenly my knees began to shake. I was busted. The familiar face belonged to Eliot Ness, Cleveland's famous Public Safety Director. His mug was plastered in the city's papers more than President Roosevelt. He looked even more distinguished in person than he did on the front page. My knees quit shaking once I sat down. Maybe he knew about the accident but at least he was not working for Mr. Fleming.

"Victor, my name's Eliot Ness and this is my

assistant, Keith Wilson. Would you like a cup of coffee or a glass of water?" The Safety Director gestured toward a nearby cabinet where a hot coffee pot sat next to a sink.

"No thank you, sir."

"Do you know who I am?"

"Yes sir, I've seen your picture in the newspapers."

"Do you know why we want to talk to you, Victor?"

"I don't think so," I stammered, expecting the worse.

"Are you sure, son?" his assistant asked me. I was dumb-founded. This was happening too fast. I just shook my head.

"Relax Victor," Ness said. "I think you're taking this the wrong way."

"We know you were involved in the accident on the Shoreway," Wilson explained.

"You don't know the whole story," I blurted out.

"You're right about that," Ness said, standing up and pouring Wilson and himself a shot of liquor. For some reason I noticed it was scotch, not bourbon. I could see the gold badge pinned to the vest inside his sports coat. "That's why we wanted to talk to you tonight. You're not in any trouble. We know you were trying to do the right thing,"

"We just need to hear your side of the story," Wilson added.

They were teaming up on me and I was feeling

threatened. I did not know where to begin or how much to tell them.

"Did Mr. Friedrich set this up?" I suddenly felt betrayed by my favorite teacher.

"Yes he did," Ness tried to explain. "But he was doing you a favor. You see, Victor, what we really need is your help."

"My help?"

"Yes." Ness sat down again and took a sip from his shot glass. Wilson followed his lead. "We know all about Mr. Fleming, thanks to Mr. Friedrich. He is angry that Fleming cares more about their German homeland and The Third Reich, than the United States."

"Mr. Friedrich knew about Mr. Fleming?"

"Yes."

"Then why didn't he tell me?"

"He was afraid you might blow his cover."

"His cover?"

"Yes, Mr. Friedrich is helping us keep tabs on Mr. Fleming."

"He is?"

"Yes, that's why he asked you to write the story about him," Wilson explained. "He hoped you might spook him into showing his hand."

"How much do you know about Mr. Fleming?" I asked them.

"More than you do," Wilson said. "At least we think we do."

"That's why you need to tell us what you know," Ness explained. "And we need to know about the accident on the Shoreway," he pointed to *The Tatler* galley sheet. "We know there is more to that story than even your principal, Mr. Tuck, knows."

"Maybe I'll try that cup of coffee," I said and the famous Safety Director who cured Chicago of Al Capone rose up from his chair and poured me a cup of printing press java.

It was the first cup of coffee I ever drank in my life. In our modest household only my father and mother could afford to drink it. We were given warm milk or a cup of tea on winter evenings to warm our bellies. Besides, with the war going on coffee was rationed just like gasoline and rubber tires.

As I sipped the coffee my heart began to race from the caffeine. Slowly I started to tell my story, how I'd been following Mr. Fleming and what I discovered about him. My lips began to move faster as I spilled my guts. The words tumbled out of my mouth, one after another. It felt great to finally blurt it all out. It was like a great weight was being lifted from my shoulders.

Surprisingly, most of my information was not news to the two lawmen. They had also been following Mr.

Fleming. They knew about his Nazi radio club and his plan to blow up the bomber plant.

They were watching him as he sent his information across Lake Erie to Canada. Ness explained to me that Fleming used the same guys who brought bootleg liquor into Cleveland from Canada during Prohibition to deliver his messages. They told me that Fleming was sending blueprints of Cleveland's buildings to his Canadian contacts. They even watched me and Doris watch him. That made me feel a little uneasy, remembering how we sat in the car afterwards.

Ness and Wilson even guessed that we were involved in the car crash on the Shoreway.

"Would you be willing to testify against the other young men in the radio club if it came down to it?" Ness asked me solemnly.

"I guess," I said softly, my heart finally beginning to slow down.

"Hopefully, it will not come to that," Wilson said.

"You see, Victor," Ness stood up again and went to the office window to look out at the printing presses. "We know that Fleming cannot blow up the bomber plant with a bunch of high school students. He is just using those kids as pawns to do his dirty work. We need to find out who is financing his operation. We must discover who gives him his orders and how he plans to do it before it is too late."

"We don't have much time," Wilson emphasized. "That's why we need your help."

I looked from Eliot Ness' face to Keith Wilson's. There was a certain gravity about their composure that I could not fathom.

"What do you want me to do?" I asked them.

CHAPTER TWENTY FIVE: The Senior Play

The next school day after my meeting with Eliot Ness I was on another assignment for *The Tatler*. I had to stay after school to visit the set of the senior class play. Our in-house thespians were tackling the 1938 Pulitzer Prize winner, *Our Town* by Thornton Wilder.

The West Tech auditorium was right off one of the main entrances to the school on the corner of West 93rd and Willard Avenues. As most of the student body streamed out the big doors into the streets I turned into the auditorium.

A couple of student actors were already on the stage practicing their lines. Other students were adjusting the lighting from the balcony. The stagehands were painting a plywood wall that would be used as a backdrop. The auditorium was bustling with activity.

I was trying to find Mr. Jorgensen, the play's faculty advisor. So I asked Pat O'Leary, Tech's reigning leading man, if he had seen him. O'Leary was the star of all the school plays over the past two years. He was pacing the stage, reading a script and was none too happy that I interrupted him. I quizzed him standing by the front row of the seats below the stage.

"Mr. Jorgensen can be found backstage working with the prop crew," O'Leary answered in a loud voice, pointing his hand with a grand sweep as if he were acting in a Shakespearean production.

"Thank you, sir." I bowed with one hand on my belt buckle, playing the role of an English servant.

O'Leary laughed at my gesture and went back to pacing the stage. This worked out well because I was looking for a reason to go backstage. I climbed the steps to the stage, circled around the actors and found my way through the various props.

Mr. Jorgensen was holding a large drawing, showing a couple male students in work clothes how he wanted the scenes set up. I stood and watched for a minute, not wanting to interrupt him, as I surveyed my surroundings. He was too busy to pay any attention to me.

It was my first time on West Tech's stage and I was bowled over by all the empty seats staring at me. I could not believe how many there were. Plus there was a large balcony. It looked like a movie theatre. I suddenly appreciated the guts it took to act in front of such a large audience.

Our Town used a sparse set so the stage crew had a

pretty easy time of it. A couple ladders and chairs were being moved into position. I walked around behind Mr. Jorgensen to look at a storage area hidden by a big curtain. There was a mishmash of props leftover from previous productions that I assumed were being saved for future plays. On the edge of the pile I noticed a bedroom set and mattress set up on their ends.

Bingo! I had hit the jackpot.

Mr. Jorgensen finally noticed me snooping around.

"May I help you?" he asked icily with a touch of his Norwegian accent.

I told him I was assigned to do a story about the upcoming senior class play for *The Tatler*. He told me it was a bad time to talk and asked if I could come back another time.

No problem, I said, and asked him if I could look around backstage. I told him that I wanted to write a different article than the usual synopsis of the senior play, maybe a story about the stage crew. No problem, he said.

Behind West Tech's auditorium there were all kinds of little rooms and stairways. Some went up for a couple of stories to where the lighting crew strung the spotlights. There was a little room off to the side that had a small kitchen with a sink. I assumed that it was a teacher's office or a resting spot for the actors. Then another stairway went down to an outside door that was only to be used as a fire escape.

I must have walked past that door a hundred times going down Willard Avenue but never noticed it because it was below ground level. To use it you would have to walk behind some big shrubs and go down some steps.

I planned on using it. When no one was around I pushed the door open from the inside. I tried pushing the latch down from the outside as I held it open but it was locked. So I pushed a little button on the edge of the door that unlocked it.

I stepped outside and took a breath of fresh air to calm my shaking hands. Then I tried going back inside. It worked, the door stayed open.

I retraced my steps, thanked Mr. Jorgensen for his hospitality, bowed good-bye to Pat O'Leary and went out the auditorium the way I came in.

Phase one of Mr. Ness' game plan was in place. My assignment was to hide in the school overnight to spy on the radio club's late night secret meeting.

The FBI was aware of the radio traffic coming from the school after hours. They could listen to Tech's radio club messages. The U.S. government had set up a secret radio station in Canada for the sole purpose of listening to radio traffic coming across the border. But the West Tech messages were in code and they had not yet broken the code. So they closed down the school's station in the name of national security. Other school stations across the country were also being shut down. However, in Tech's case, the real reason was to stop the messages and maybe spook the radio club into revealing their secrets before they closed down.

Mr. Ness hoped that I might hear some conversations that would reveal their plans in more detail. He also wanted me to try to take a second look inside Mr. Fleming's cabinet. I had told him about my key. Mr. Ness hoped that I might find the club's codebook, sneak it out for them to copy, replace it and then compare it with their conversations with Germany that they had been recording. It was a long shot but worth the gamble.

I was the perfect tool for their plans because if the janitor or a teacher caught me inside the school after classes I could just claim that I fell asleep after class and was locked inside the school by mistake. If one of Ness' agents were spotted inside the school their cover would be blown.

It was a risky assignment but I agreed to do it for my country and even more importantly for Doris' sake. I did not like Mr. Fleming's hold over her family. Mr. Ness told me that if I landed in any trouble he would clear things with Mr. Tuck.

The radio club was supposed to meet the tenth period after school just like the other school clubs. So their meeting should be over by four o'clock. But the

FBI had picked up Tech's radio traffic as late as 6 p.m. That meant they were staying in the building long after everyone else had gone home.

My plan was to sneak back into the school after classes let out and hide out in the backstage of the auditorium. If something happened and I was somehow locked in I would spend the night sleeping on the mattress in the prop area. Then in the morning I would just report to class once the regular students entered the building.

I told my parents that I was spending the evening at Frank's home to work on a school project. It was not too much of a stretch of the truth.

Sneaking back into the school was almost too easy. I walked up and down Willard Avenue a couple of times until the coast was clear then bolted behind the shrubs in front of the door I had left unlocked. It was still unlocked. I walked into the stage area that was now abandoned.

My heart was racing so I sat on a stage sofa to catch my breath. I thought about Doris. I had not seen her since our fateful New Year's Eve date. Eliot Ness said they would watch out for her and keep her out of school on the pretext that her illness was serious. That would keep her out of harm's way until Mr. Fleming could be brought to justice. I trusted Mr. Ness but still missed Doris' company and advice.

Then suddenly the lights were turned off in most of the auditorium. I could hear more lights clicking off down the hallways. I figured it was the janitor locking the school down for the evening.

I wondered how Mr. Fleming managed to stay in the school after hours. I knew there was night school for students who dropped out and were trying to obtain their degrees the hard way but I also knew they were held in only a small area of the building.

Maybe Mr. Fleming was paying off Lazarus, the janitor. Times were hard back then and for a couple bucks you could buy almost anything, even allegiance to your country.

It was past my usual dinnertime so I pulled a sandwich out of my jacket pocket that I had made for the occasion. Eating it made me thirsty so I went looking for the nearest water fountain out in the lobby. I knew where most of them were located after three years of walking around the building.

But first I had to check the hallways to make sure they were clear. I opened the auditorium door just a hair, looked both ways, then made my way to the first floor drinking fountain near the principal's office. I was suddenly afraid that Mr. Tuck might be working late. Who knew when he went home? He treated the school like it was his personal baby so maybe he stayed there all night himself.

While I was taking a long drink I suddenly heard footsteps coming my way. There was nowhere to hide except in Mr. Tuck's office. What a dilemma. But I had no choice. His door was open so I scooted inside. I felt like I was committing blasphemy. It was like hiding under the altar at church.

As I stood by the door I could hear the footsteps of a group of students. I could hear them talking among themselves. Then I caught a German word. Then a German sentence. It had to be the radio club. What a close call. I stood perfectly still until they walked by.

I took a quick look around Mr. Tuck's office. It was like invading the inner sanctum. There were a few pictures of his family, the principal with his wife and children and a picture of him boxing in his youth. You don't think about a principal's personal life when you are a high school student but there it was. It was a bit shocking but I did not have time to digest the information. The game was afoot.

The radio club met in the small fourth floor classroom that housed their equipment. I had already scouted out the surroundings. I would stay in the band room next to it and listen to them through a clean air vent. The vent was just off the floor, covered by a metal screen. If you lay down on the floor you could look through the screen and see a section of their classroom.

I heard them go up the steps and close a door

behind them. Once the coast was clear I snuck into the band room. There was a lot of noise going on in the radio club room.

I could hear them tinkering with their transmitter and receiver. They were talking in both English and German and some of their discussion was too technical for me to understand. Mr. Fleming told someone to adjust the wire attached to the antenna on the roof of the building. Suddenly there was a crackling sound.

It sounded like a twisting of dials. The crackling died down and a voice came from far away. I lay perfectly still on the floor, trying to catch a glimpse of the operation.

Then someone started tapping out a message in Morse code. I'd learned it once as a kid but never kept up with it so I could not understand what they were saying. It was probably in code anyway.

When the telegraphing ceased a German voice came out of nowhere. It was scratchy but audible. The stranger said a few sentences. Mr. Fleming answered the voice in fluent German.

I was suddenly stunned by the enormity of it all. Was it really possible for some high school kids in Cleveland, Ohio to talk to a stranger on the other side of Lake Erie over radio waves? I never appreciated the potential of a ham radio before. It was as amazing as Dick Tracy's two-way wrist radio.

Mr. Fleming talked to the German-Canadian for a few minutes in his native tongue. So I still had little information to pass on to Mr. Ness. I was beginning to feel like a failure. Mr. Fleming ended his conversation with a pleasant Auf Wiedersehen, followed by a curt "Heil Hitler."

The "Heil Hitler" caught my immediate attention. I was in shock. I continued to listen, afraid to move a muscle for fear of being discovered.

"Now that our mission is accomplished let the meeting begin," Mr. Fleming addressed the group. "Since the federal government is taking away our call letters we must decide on our next course of action."

"Screw the feds," one of the boys shouted and everyone laughed.

"Now, now, my little Feurers," Mr. Fleming also laughed. "We are not the only target of their wrath. They are shutting down amateur ham radios all across the country."

"Can't we continue to operate secretly?" a student asked.

"Yes, make up our own call letters?" another wondered.

"No, that is too risky," Mr. Fleming explained. "As long as we are simply a student club just practicing our radio skills communicating with Canada, we have nothing to fear."

"Except fear itself," a boy screamed and everyone laughed again.

"Yes, you mock President Roosevelt and with good reason." Mr. Fleming joined in the fun. "His days are numbered. And thanks to your efforts The Third Reich will one day stretch its power over the Atlantic Ocean, onto the shores of America."

"Heil Hitler, Heil Hitler," a couple of the boys cheered. I could hear their chairs grinding against the tile as they stood up. Then I could see their shadows on the floor, holding their arms out straight in the Nazi salute. I suddenly imagined what they would do to me if they found out that I was eavesdropping on them.

"All right, boys, let us proceed with the meeting. Who is going to take home the different parts of the apparatus? We must hide them in case we need them in the future."

Various students volunteered to harbor sections of the radio setup. Then Mr. Fleming explained some maintenance procedures for the equipment, thanked them for their efforts and officially announced that the West Tech Radio Club was disbanded until further notice.

"The next time we meet," Mr. Fleming continued with a somber voice, "will be at Gate A of Cleveland Municipal Airport. As usual keep your eye on page three of *The Tatler*. We will continue to use the ad for Kluck's Automotive to announce the date of our meeting."

Mr. Fleming had been using *The Tatler*, my newspaper, to pass secret messages to his troops. Somehow I felt violated.

"We go from there to the bomber plant?" one of the students asked.

"That is our plan," Mr. Fleming said. "We will strike a glorious blow for The Third Reich."

This time the "Heil Hitlers" came fast and furious as the whole group began to shout.

"Quiet, quiet," Mr. Fleming raised his voice above theirs but you could hear the satisfaction in his voice. "We must not be heard, we have come much too far to lose our way now."

The meeting ended after the radio club students sang a song in German. I stayed on the floor, holding my breath as I watched their shoes file by underneath the band room door. My mission was accomplished. I did not find the date of the bombing plan but I knew where to find it.

My heart was beating so loudly in my chest that I could not move until it quieted down. After the last footstep fell silent I finally stood up, brushed my clothes off and sat at an empty desk.

I had to plan my next move. Should I follow the

radio club out the door and hurry to Mr. Ness with my information? Or should I try to break into Mr. Fleming's cabinet one last time to search for the secret codebook?

I was angry and greedy. I decided to go for the whole ball of wax.

CHAPTER TWENTY SIX:
The Chase

West Tech's hallways were empty as I made my way up to Mr. Fleming's chemistry classroom. I expected some activity from the night classes but maybe there were none scheduled that evening. Maybe they met for only a few nights a week. I never paid much attention to them. They were just something you heard about when a teacher threatened to fail someone.

"You'll have to come back to night school if you want to graduate," was one of the tools the teachers used to enforce discipline. By threatening expulsion they could turn a problem teen's behavior around 180 degrees. Going to school during the day and enjoying your evenings sounded lot better than trying to earn your diploma at night school after a hard day's work.

The quiet halls brought back memories of the early morning job I had sophomore year. Rick Lopez and I helped Lazarus, the custodian, pull a wooden flat-bedded cart around the empty halls before school started.

The only sound we heard was the clattering of the metal wheels as we shipped supplies to the various shops and classrooms.

It was only an hour every morning but it added up to five hours a week, twenty hours a month. A nice little paycheck for a fifteen-year-old kid. It made me quite a bit richer than most of my peers. Plus it helped me learn many of Tech's nooks and crannies.

The door to Mr. Fleming's classroom was unlocked. It struck me that all the classroom doors were unlocked. I guessed that there was no real reason to lock them. The school was obviously pretty secure at night and there was little inside them for anyone to steal.

Except for Mr. Fleming's cabinet. I slowly closed the door behind me, then fumbled around in my pocket for the duplicate key that the shop guys had made for me. It was not in my right front pants pocket, the one where I carried everything, including my cash and change.

I had a panic attack. Did it fall out while I was lying down on the band room floor? I quickly searched my other pockets. Fortunately, I found it in my rear pants pocket. I guess I put it there so I would not lose it but I forgot it was there.

I began to worry that I was losing my mind. The stress of all this spying was beginning to take its toll. I vowed that after I looked in Mr. Fleming's cabinet that I would be done with the whole thing. I was in over my head and enough was enough. I did my part for my country but that was it. Besides, I missed Doris.

I slowly tried to turn the key. At first it would not turn so I panicked again. Maybe Mr. Fleming had changed the lock. But after applying a little pressure it finally clicked. I forgot that it was not a perfect fit.

The door opened and the blueprints were still there. This time I could take my time and look at them. I was going to spread them out on Mr. Fleming's desk and see just what he had been saving. But first I took all the rolls out and looked for a codebook. Of course, what a codebook looked like I had no idea. I turned on his desk lamp for more light.

Underneath the rolls I found a couple of books that looked like journals. My heart started beating fast again. I hoped that I was too young to have a heart attack. The first one had "West Tech Radio Club" printed on its cover.

I thought I had discovered the Holy Grail. But when I opened it all I found was the names of the club members and some notes about the meetings. I was about to open the second journal when the door suddenly began to open.

I prayed that it was Mr. Lazarus again. No such luck. This time it was Mr. Fleming. He turned on the classroom lights and suddenly our eyes met. He was as surprised to see me as I was to see him. But he kept his cool.

"Mr. Blazek, what are you doing here?" he asked me slowly, choosing his words very carefully. He was still standing in the doorway, his eyes searching the desk where I had his blueprints and journals spread out.

"I was wondering the same thing about you, Mr. Fleming." I answered with a false sense of bravado.

For a minute I was intimidated because he was a teacher. I had always been trained to respect my teachers. But then I remembered the Radio Club meeting that I just witnessed and I became angry. Angry that he was a traitor, angry that he was betraying his country, angry that he tried to kill Doris and me.

"This is my classroom, I have the right to be here," Mr. Fleming said as he shut the door behind him. "You on the other hand could be expelled for being in here."

He began to walk toward his desk as I backed away from it. He looked down at the blueprints and journals. "Find anything interesting?" he asked me.

I knew that there was no time to talk to him. I bolted past him and opened the door. He turned quickly and tried to grab me but I pulled away from him and ran out into the hallway. I instinctively ran toward the nearest stairway at the rear of the building.

Mr. Fleming followed me but he was no match for my speed. I was younger than him and in much better shape. I hit the stairs and jumped down them three steps at a time. I was experienced at running Tech's stairways. It was the way we trained for the wrestling team during the bad weather months. I had run up and down those stairs so many times I knew each loose piece of tile by heart.

But I was moving too fast. I almost tripped and twisted my ankle. It was a wake up call. I would have to sacrifice a little speed for safety. If I hurt myself he would catch up with me for sure. I lost him on the steps and made it to the back door but the door was locked with chains from the inside, I guessed that was how they secured the building at night.

Now what? There had to be an exit somewhere. I was in the basement so I headed for the auto shop. I could hear Mr. Fleming following me. He could hear my footsteps just like I could hear his.

I ran through the parked cars the students worked on like I was running across a crowded highway, dodging cars and toolboxes and mufflers lying on the ground. I found the back door that connected the auto shop with the greenhouse. It was locked with chains also.

Damn it. Mr. Fleming caught up with me in the auto shop. He was breathing heavily so he slowed down the chase.

"I believe you are trapped, Mr. Blazek." We were both puffing but I was puffing louder and harder. He had taken his time like a relentless wolf stalking a rabbit.

I looked around and grabbed a wrench off a tool

shelf. "Stay away from me, Mr. Fleming," I ordered him. "I don't want to hurt you."

"You won't hurt me and I won't hurt you," he stopped in his tracks surveying the situation. "I just want to talk to you."

"I have nothing to say to you."

"Why did you break into my cabinet?" he asked me.

Suddenly he picked something off the floor. At first I could not see what it was. He kept his hand hidden behind a nearby Packard.

He started to walk toward me and I circled behind a car away from him. Then I saw what he had picked up. It was a tire iron that was used to change the lug nuts on flat tires. But it was not the crossed one with four sizes that looks like an X. It was the single bolt style, a long straight cast iron rod that curved near the small knob on its end.

Mr. Fleming had trumped my wrench. The tire iron was a more formidable weapon than my puny hand wrench. It was like me using a bow and arrow against his rifle. He had me backed into a corner and I did not like the odds.

I kept looking for a way out but could not find one. If I tried to run past him he could knock me out with his tire iron.

"Stay back and we'll talk," I told him. I was trying to buy some time.

He stopped. "One last time, what were you doing in my classroom?"

I knew he was just trying to find out as much as he could before he put me away. I knew he was a dangerous man. I could not hope to deal with him but I needed to figure out a way to escape.

"If I tell you will you put down the tire iron?"

He put the tire iron on the hood of a nearby car. It was my brother Andy's Ford Roadster. I could not believe it. A few days earlier I had brought it into the shop so they could fix the damage from the New Year's Eve accident. If only Mr. Fleming knew.

"Okay," I looked around frantically. "I was mad at you because you wouldn't give me more information for my *Tatler* story. So I decided to take matters into my own hands."

I could tell by the look on his face that he was not buying my story but he kept questioning me. "Is that why you went to the Haufbrau House?"

"The Haufbrau House?" I was really stalling now. "The Haufbrau House? I was listening to the band. Is there something wrong with that?"

Then it hit me, I saw my way out. I began to move sideways. He picked up the tire iron again.

"It depends on why you were really there," he said.

I had noticed the overhead doors that were on the Willard Avenue side of the school. I used them to bring my brother Andy's car inside the auto shop.

"Why do you think I was there?" I asked him. I slowly moved toward the latch that freed an overhead weight that pulled open the door.

"You were following me, Mr. Blazek. Do you think I am a fool?" He walked between two cars.

"Yes!" I hollered at him. I pulled the door latch. In a flash he knew what I was doing. As he ran around the car the overhead door began to rise. I rolled on the ground under the door not waiting for it to open all the way. Mr. Fleming ran toward me but he was too slow.

He was not spry enough to repeat my tactic but he did crouch under the door as it began to rise. He was still carrying the tire iron as he stood up on the outside of the building, the overhead door rising behind him.

He knew he could not catch me. He wanted to see in what direction I was running. He still had hopes of jumping into his car and chasing me down. Instead he was surprised by an unexpected figure.

"Mr. Fleming." A tall, lean man in a long winter coat said to him. They were eyeball to eyeball. Another much larger man stood behind the stranger. "I'm Eliot Ness. Let's have that tire iron."

CHAPTER TWENTY SEVEN: The Trap

The following Wednesday there was an ad on page three of *The Tatler*. "TIRE SALE at Kluck Automotive, One Day Only, January 17 after 7 pm." I noticed it because I put it there, following the directions of Eliot Ness.

Mr. Fleming had mysteriously disappeared from his chemistry class duties. The official word that his substitute gave his students was that he was suddenly called out of town due to a family illness.

The radio club members had to be confused. They probably figured that he was either lying low before the big event or needed to go to Canada for further instructions.

The truth was that the FBI had taken him to Washington for questioning. And Eliot Ness asked me for one last favor. By planting the ad in *The Tatler* he hoped to gather some hard evidence against his student accomplices and maybe learn a little more about Mr. Fleming's plans in case he was a bit reluctant to spill his guts.

The radio club was more than just Nazi supporters. If Ness could bust them with explosives at the airport he could make a serious case for an espionage charge against Fleming and come down harder on the boys even if they were juveniles.

Once again I was asked to be the fall guy. Ness wanted me to show up at the airport with a message from Mr. Fleming. When they asked me why I was working for Mr. Fleming I was supposed to tell them that I was in on the plan from the beginning.

January 17 was a cold, snowy day in Cleveland. I was not sure how the other members of the radio club planned on going to the airport. Maybe they would take a trolley or be dropped off by unsuspecting friends or relatives.

As for me I was driving in style. For once I did not have to borrow a car. Eliot Ness provided one for me.

My job was to lead a three-car caravan. Another student about my age, who also worked for Ness, drove the car behind me. Ness and a few of his Cleveland "Untouchables" followed behind us in the third car.

We parked in the area reserved for taxicabs until a few minutes after seven. I rehearsed my story to myself a few times, wondering if I would be able to make myself sound convincing.

When Ness honked the horn in his car it was my

signal to drive up to Gate A in the new arrivals section of the airport. I pulled up to the curb and then jumped out of my car, leaving the motor running. A skycap walked up to me and asked me where I was going.

"I have to meet someone inside," I told him.

"You can't leave your car there, you'll get a ticket."

"Sorry, I'll just have to chance it."

I ran inside the airport and looked around. At first I did not see anyone from the radio club. So I walked around a little bit until I spotted Fritz Gottlieb standing by the baggage area. It must have been their pre-arranged meeting area.

"Hello Fritz," I said firmly and shook his hand. Inside I was shaking in my boots.

"Slats?" he was surprised to see me. "What are you doing here?"

"Mr. Fleming sent me," I said quietly, looking over my shoulder as if it was a big secret. The other members of the club surrounded us.

"You!" Fritz said loudly. "Mr. Fleming said you were spying on us."

"I was working for him, you idiot. Keep your voice down."

Fritz had a very confused look on his face. His friend Axel Wagner spoke up. "What were you doing for him?"

"I was spying on you guys, what do you think? He

was making sure that none of you turned chicken. Do you have the stuff?"

"Right here," a student I did not know picked up his suitcase. A couple other students did likewise.

"This is no place to talk," I said softly but firmly. "I've got a couple cars outside to take us over to the bomber plant."

"Where's Mr. Fleming?" Fritz asked.

"He's already over there, setting up the detonator."

The group of German radio club members looked at each other. They did not know what to make of me. They seemed torn between running away and getting on with their task. I knew that they felt strongly about their views and that they had worked on their plan for a long time. I could see their grips tightening around their suitcases with the explosives inside them. I knew that I needed one more argument to convince them that I was for real.

"Come on you guys, Mr. Fleming's waiting for you," I cajoled them. "Are you going to leave him hanging after all he's done for you?"

Fritz looked at me real hard, trying to read my facial expression. He was trying to decide if I was telling the truth.

"All right, let's go," Fritz spoke for the group. He picked up his briefcase and walked toward the exit gate. The others followed his lead. I walked next to Fritz to show him where I was parked.

But just as we approached the glass doors Fritz stopped. "Hey, it's a cop!" he shouted.

"What?" I said. Ness was supposed to wait until I put them in the car with the explosives.

It was not Eliot Ness. It was a traffic cop giving my car a ticket. The skycap must have ratted me out.

"Hold on, don't panic," I told the club. "I'll handle this." I walked outside and left them standing in the lobby. They could watch me through the glass doors.

I walked out to the car. "Sorry officer," I said. "This is my car."

"A pretty nice ride for a kid your age," he looked at me suspiciously as he wrote down the license plate numbers. "Do you have your driver's license?"

"Yes, sir." I pulled it out of my wallet. "I'm just picking up a group of friends from school."

"What school?" He looked at me suspiciously, just like Fritz Gottlieb did. This time the answer came easier.

"West Tech."

"Oh yeah, is Tuck still there?" he asked me. I could tell it was more of a test question than a friendly inquiry.

"Oh yeah, still as tough as nails."

"Okay kid," the cop smiled. "I can't give you a break on the ticket because I already wrote it. But pick up your friends in a hurry or I'll have to call a tow truck."

"Yes, sir. They're right inside."

At least I hoped that they were. They were standing around with their backs to the cop. Only Fritz had been glancing over at us every now and then.

"What was that all about?" Fritz asked me when I joined them.

"Just a parking ticket." I waved it in front of them. "He says we have to move out fast or he'll tow my car."

The fact that the cop gave me a hard time actually had a positive effect on the radio club members. It reinforced my claim that I was on their side, that I could be trusted.

"Okay, let's move out." Fritz once again took the lead. Maybe he was the club president.

As I walked outside I waved to the other Ness car driven by the student. He pulled up as I opened the trunk.

"Who's that?" Fritz asked suspiciously. He was loading his heavy suitcase into the trunk.

"I don't know the guy. Mr. Fleming sent another car to help carry all the stuff."

"He's probably our ride out of here," Axel told Fritz.

"Oh yeah," Fritz admitted. "I forgot about that."

Fritz, Axel and another student named Dolph, who I didn't know, jumped into my car. Fritz told the other guys to jump into the car behind us. Once were all packed in we moved out.

Eliot Ness had given me a dry run. He gave me a pass to go inside the bomber plant gate. Once inside the fences they would not be able to escape. But I was to take my time and try to pump them for information. It was a risky business because I was supposed to be in on the plot already. Ness suggested that I just ask open-ended questions and see what they revealed.

"Mr. Fleming gave us passes to get through the gates," I told them.

"He thinks of everything," Fritz said.

"This is going to be great," Axel added.

"Which car are we parking by the building?" Fritz asked me.

"I think it's this one, Mr. Fleming will make the call."

"Kind of a nice ride to be blowing up," Fritz said.

"It'll be magnificent to watch," Dolph said.

"We should be long gone," Fritz corrected him. "Only Mr. Fleming gets to see it from behind the fence."

"Did you bring enough stuff?" I asked Fritz.

"Why do you keep calling it stuff?" Fritz asked me. "There's enough dynamite in those suitcases to make us all disappear."

"I'm still practicing talking around strangers," I explained. Actually, I did not know what they had in those suitcases and now that I knew I wish that I didn't.

"What's our cover anyway?" Fritz asked as we approached the gate.

"We're looking for work," I answered.

"This time of night?" Axel asked.

"They work three shifts out here," I did some quick thinking. "Mr. Fleming says the pass won't be a problem."

A guard in Army uniform stopped us. I rolled down the window and handed him the pass Eliot Ness gave me. He looked at it for a few very long seconds.

"Use the parking lot on the right," he ordered us.

Then he went back into the gatehouse and pushed a button that raised the bar blocking the entrance.

"Mr. Fleming does think of everything," Axel echoed Fritz's familiar refrain. I pulled up and waited for the second car to come through the gate.

"That was almost too easy." Dolph laughed.

"We're supposed to meet Mr. Fleming over by the fence," I told my passengers. I drove real slowly, watching the mirror to make sure that not only the car following me made it through the gate but also Mr. Ness' car. "Look for a 1938 Buick Sedan."

I drove around the perimeter of the parking lot. It was already dark outside and the snow was blowing in swirls.

"I don't see him," Fritz said, pressing his head against the window.

I did not answer him. I parked the car in the pre-arranged location and waited for the car behind me to pull up alongside of us. Then I rolled down the window. Bruno Stark, another football player, rolled down his window on the front passenger side of the other car.

"Where's Mr. Fleming?" he asked me.

"He should be here," I said, sticking my head out the window. I saw Eliot Ness pulling up in his car. There were two more cars behind his and an Army Jeep. "There he is." I pointed at Ness's car. Then I opened my car door and walked toward the oncoming vehicles. The teenage driver of the car next to me did likewise.

As the Ness cavalcade approached I just kept walking past it. Eliot Ness stuck his hand out of his car window and I handed him my car keys. The last car stopped and I jumped inside. The radio club members were surrounded before they knew what hit them.

Ness' assistant, Keith Wilson, was driving my car. As we left I could see the Army guys opening the two trunks, inspecting the contents with their flashlights.

"Nice job," Wilson told me.

"No sweat," I told him. It was a big lie. I looked at my hands. They were dripping with perspiration.

"I thought that traffic cop was going to blow the

whole operation." He laughed.

"Me, too."

"Are you hungry? Would you like to stop anywhere on the way home?"

"Could we drive by Doris' house? I'd like to tell her that it's over."

CHAPTER TWENTY-EIGHT: The West Tech Relays

It was a fine, sunny Saturday afternoon in May of 1942. Doris and I were sitting in the stands normally used to watch football games. Instead we were watching the West Tech Relays. We were lucky to find a couple of good seats. The stands were packed with fans. Even the areas surrounding the racetrack that circled the football field were filled with wall-to-wall spectators. It was standing room only.

Twenty-eight high school teams from Northeast Ohio were competing in a wide variety of track and field events. It was the prestigious track meet in Cuyahoga County.

It had been four months since "the bomber plant incident," as we referred to it. Because of the war, or national security, or whatever you wanted to call it, we knew little about what happened to the radio club students or Mr. Fleming. All Doris and I knew was that they were no longer attending West Tech.

Her grandparents had been secreted out of Germany and were now living with her parents on the west side of Cleveland.

We were enjoying the lovely spring afternoon, talking to our friends, joking about our upcoming graduation and cheering on the West Tech track team when a familiar face came walking up the stairway between the seats. It was Eliot Ness.

"Hello, Victor," he smiled. "May I join you?"

"Mr. Ness, are you kidding?"

"Move over, Victor," Doris said. "Make some room for him."

"That's all right," Eliot Ness said. "How about if we take a walk?"

I looked over at Doris then back to Mr. Ness, wondering if he meant her also. "You, too, Doris," Eliot picked up on my dilemma.

I guessed that he did not want anyone around us to eavesdrop on our conversation.

"Everything all right, Mr. Ness?" I asked him once we made our way down the steps.

"Fine, fine," Mr. Ness said, not quite answering my question. His mind seemed to be occupied elsewhere. "I figure I owe you an update on our case."

We were mingling with the standing room crowd around the outside of the track. Before the safety director could explain his visit an off-duty policeman working security at the Relays noticed him. "Hello, Director. How do you like your new job?"

"Hey, Sam." He shook the cop's hand. "I'm looking forward to it."

He kept walking without explaining the conversation so I asked him about it. "You have a new position?"

"It's not official yet but I'm leaving the city to work for the feds on the war effort. In a way I have you to thank for the promotion."

"Me?"

"Yes, Victor. J. Edgar Hoover himself was impressed by our capturing Mr. Fleming. He was an even bigger threat than we realized."

"Really?" Doris asked.

"Yes, Doris. You have a lot to thank Victor for yourself. You were caught up in a very tough crowd."

"Don't I know it." Doris took my hand.

We weaved through the spectators, saying hi to our fellow students, most of whom did not recognize Eliot Ness in real life.

"I didn't come here to talk about myself," Mr. Ness said. "Before I leave for Washington I wanted to ask Victor what we could do to repay him for his efforts. Any ideas, Victor?"

"I would like to know what happened to Mr. Fleming and the radio club guys. Unless it's top secret or something."

"I did promise you an update," Ness said. "Mr. Fleming is in a federal penitentiary. He is going to be in there for a very long time. And the students have all been sent to a prison camp out west. No use having them wasting away in a prison cell. They'll be doing hard labor until the war is over. By that time their minds should be straightened out."

"Jeepers," Doris said.

"Do their parents know?" I asked.

"Oh, yes, but they are probably too embarrassed to say anything."

"Geez," I said.

"Victor," Ness began. "You really did a great favor for your country. We want to do something for you in return. You think about it and let me know. But you only have a few days to decide because I'm going to Washington D.C. next week and I'm not sure when I'll be back."

By this time we had circled the West Tech track and were on the school side of the perimeter fence. We stopped right in front of the pole vault event and the three of us leaned over the fence to watch it.

"I don't know what to say," I told Eliot Ness.

"Did you ever run track?" he asked me, changing the subject.

"No, I'm a wrestler. But not a very good one."

"That's how I was with track," Eliot laughed. "But it

never mattered to me, I just enjoyed the competition."

"I know what you mean."

"Me, too," Doris added. "I love roller skating. I don't even care about the trophies."

We watched the pole vaulters in silence for a few minutes.

"You know, Mr. Ness, there is something I've been thinking about," I told him.

"What's that?"

"I doubt if you can do anything about it, but you know I am going to be drafted when I graduate."

"You want me to help get you out of the draft?" he asked in disbelief.

"No, not at all," I was shocked that he would even suggest such a thing. "I'd like to be an Army paratrooper."

"You would?" Doris asked. "You never mentioned that to me."

"Just something I've been thinking about," I told her.

"Sounds pretty dangerous to me," Eliot Ness said. "Why would you want to do that?"

"My cousin Joe is training with the 101st Airborne out of Fort Benning, Georgia," I explained. "I read a few of his letters home. I think it would be pretty exciting, jumping out of an airplane. Besides, I hear they pay you more for it."

"I wouldn't jump out of a plane for the money," Ness laughed. "The Army's pay scale isn't even enough to live on. What would you do with the extra money?"

The safety director caught me off guard with that question. "Just give it to my mom. She's going to have it tough when I leave. She'll still have three mouths to feed at home."

We watched in awe as a pole vaulter crashed against the bar and landed hard onto the rubber cushion. I was waiting for Mr. Ness to respond but he did not say anything. He just watched as the pole vaulter slowly picked himself up off the ground.

"That might be you bouncing off the ground with your parachute," he finally laughed. He turned and shook my hand. "Well, we'll see what we can do, Victor. You'll have to excuse me now. I have another appointment."

Just as we were parting a hush came over the crowd nearest to us, as if a Hollywood movie star had jumped out of a limousine. I thought maybe the masses finally recognized Eliot Ness, who had a very distinguished career as Cleveland's Safety Director. But it was not Mr. Ness that the crowd recognized. Instead it was principal C.C. Tuck who was coming our way. The spectators moved out of his way as if he was Moses parting the Red Sea.

"Mr. Ness," he shook Eliot's hand as soon as he came near us.

"Mr. Tuck, I presume."

They were both a couple of larger than life person-alities. And not just because they were taller than the average citizen.

"Good-bye Doris." Ness took Doris' hand and gently covered it with his other hand. "Thanks for all your help, both of you."

Mr. Tuck squeezed the top of my shoulder blade like I was his son. "See you in school Monday, Victor."

Then the two living legends walked off together into the sunlight, back toward the hulking structure of a building that we called West Tech High School.

Why they were meeting together I never did find out. Probably another top secret government investigation. But Eliot Ness was true to his word. When I was drafted into the Army a month after graduation they told me that there was already a spot reserved for me in the 101st Airborne Division.

But that's another story.

West Technical High School,
West 93rd and Willard Avenue,
Cleveland
Sixth City

"The aim of West Technical High School is not only to train its students in different school subjects but to aid in the development of each student's personal habits and characteristics so that they will be a help rather than a hindrance when he leaves school.

I hope that the school has succeeded in helping each of you to take your place in the social and economic life of our city."

– Principal C.C. Tuck's Farewell Address
to the January, 1937 graduating class.

AUTHOR'S NOTE

I would like to offer an apology to all the West Tech graduates who may find inaccuracies in *The West Tech Terrorist*. Please note that this is a piece of historical fiction. I combined my experiences as a June, 1967 graduate with those of my father, a January, 1942 grad. I realize that some of the scenes and references in the book could not have occurred in the 1941-1942 school year. However, sometimes it is necessary to include events and ideas to make the story flow. The greatness of West Tech and its legendary principal, C. C. Tuck, was that it was basically the same school in 1967 that it was in 1942, twenty-five years later. I also owe a special thanks to all the West Tech alumni and teachers who shared their memories with me. There are too many of them to list here but I would be remiss if I did not thank Robert Kitzerow, class of 1938, for his valuable advice. I hope I was able to capture the spirit of West Tech that so many of us were fortunate enough to experience.

An aerial view of the West Tech
neighborhood, circa 1940

Author Peter Jedick's 1967 West Tech senior class photo. As class president he was asked to give a speech at the commencement ceremonies. While doing research for his speech he learned that representatives from post-World War II Germany and Japan toured the United States to learn about our education system. One of the schools they visited was Cleveland's West Technical High School. Applying the lessons they learned at West Tech helped both war torn countries build strong democratic economies.

Peter Jedick is an award-winning freelance writer. He is the author of two previous non-fiction books: *League Park* and *CLEVELAND: Where the East Coast Meets the Midwest*. This is his second novel. His first novel was *HIPPIES*.

For more information visit *www.westtechterrorist.com* and *www.hippiesbook.com*.